WHEN YOU'RE GONE

(A Finn Wright FBI Suspense Thriller—Book Seven)

BLAKE PIERCE

D1695530

Blake Pierce

Blake Pierce is the USA Today bestselling author of the RILEY PAGE mystery series, which includes seventeen books. Blake Pierce is also the author of the MACKENZIE WHITE mystery series, comprising fourteen books; of the AVERY BLACK mystery series, comprising six books; of the KERI LOCKE mystery series, comprising five books; of the MAKING OF RILEY PAIGE mystery series, comprising six books; of the KATE WISE mystery series, comprising seven books; of the CHLOE FINE psychological suspense mystery, comprising six books; of the JESSIE HUNT psychological suspense thriller series, comprising thirty-eight books (and counting); of the AU PAIR psychological suspense thriller series, comprising three books; of the ZOE PRIME mystery series, comprising six books; of the ADELE SHARP mystery series, comprising sixteen books, of the EUROPEAN VOYAGE cozy mystery series, comprising six books; of the LAURA FROST FBI suspense thriller, comprising eleven books; of the ELLA DARK FBI suspense thriller, comprising twenty-one books (and counting); of the A YEAR IN EUROPE cozy mystery series, comprising nine books, of the AVA GOLD mystery series, comprising six books; of the RACHEL GIFT mystery series, comprising fifteen books (and counting); of the VALERIE LAW mystery series, comprising nine books; of the PAIGE KING mystery series, comprising eight books; of the MAY MOORE mystery series, comprising eleven books; of the CORA SHIELDS mystery series, comprising eight books; of the NICKY LYONS mystery series, comprising eight books, of the CAMI LARK mystery series, comprising ten books; of the AMBER YOUNG mystery series, comprising eight books; of the DAISY FORTUNE mystery series, comprising five books; of the FIONA RED mystery series, comprising thirteen books (and counting); of the FAITH BOLD mystery series, comprising seventeen books (and counting); of the JULIETTE HART mystery series, comprising five books; of the MORGAN CROSS mystery series, comprising thirteen books (and counting); of the FINN WRIGHT mystery series, comprising seven books (and counting); of the SHEILA STONE suspense thriller series, comprising eight books (and counting); of the RACHEL BLACKWOOD suspense thriller series, comprising eight books (and counting); and of the new THE GOVERNESS psychological suspense thriller series, comprising five books (and counting).

An avid reader and lifelong fan of the mystery and thriller genres, Blake loves to hear from you, so please feel free to visit www.blakepierceauthor.com to learn more and stay in touch.

BOOKS BY BLAKE PIERCE

THE GOVERNESS PSYCHOLOGICAL SUSPENSE
ONE LAST LIE (Book #1)
ONE LAST SMILE (Book #2)
ONE LAST BREATH (Book #3)
ONE LAST GOODBYE (Book #4)
ONE LAST SECRET (Book #5)

RACHEL BLACKWOOD SUSPENSE THRILLER
NOT THIS WAY (Book #1)
NOT THIS TIME (Book #2)
NOT THIS CLOSE (Book #3)
NOT THIS ROAD (Book #4)
NOT THIS LATE (Book #5)
NOT THIS NIGHT (Book #6)
NOT THIS PLACE (Book #7)
NOT THIS SOON (Book #8)

SHEILA STONE SUSPENSE THRILLER
SILENT GIRL (Book #1)
SILENT TRAIL (Book #2)
SILENT NIGHT (Book #3)
SILENT HOUSE (Book #4)
SILENT SCREAM (Book #5)
SILENT PREY (Book #6)
SILENT RITUAL (Book #7)
SILENT PRAYER (Book #8)

FINN WRIGHT MYSTERY SERIES
WHEN YOU'RE MINE (Book #1)
WHEN YOU'RE SAFE (Book #2)
WHEN YOU'RE CLOSE (Book #3)
WHEN YOU'RE SLEEPING (Book #4)
WHEN YOU'RE SANE (Book #5)
WHEN YOU'RE SILENT (Book #6)
WHEN YOU'RE GONE (Book #7)

MORGAN CROSS MYSTERY SERIES
FOR YOU (Book #1)
FOR RAGE (Book #2)
FOR LUST (Book #3)
FOR WRATH (Book #4)
FOREVER (Book #5)
FOR US (Book #6)
FOR NOW (Book #7)
FOR ONCE (Book #8)
FOR ETERNITY (Book #9)
FORLORN (Book #10)
FOR SILENCE (Book #11)
FORBIDDEN (Book #12)
FOR FEAR (Book #13)
FORSAKEN (Book #14)

JULIETTE HART MYSTERY SERIES
NOTHING TO FEAR (Book #1)
NOTHING THERE (Book #2)
NOTHING WATCHING (Book #3)
NOTHING HIDING (Book #4)
NOTHING LEFT (Book #5)

FAITH BOLD MYSTERY SERIES
SO LONG (Book #1)
SO COLD (Book #2)
SO SCARED (Book #3)
SO NORMAL (Book #4)
SO FAR GONE (Book #5)
SO LOST (Book #6)
SO ALONE (Book #7)
SO FORGOTTEN (Book #8)
SO INSANE (Book #9)
SO SMITTEN (Book #10)
SO SIMPLE (Book #11)
SO BROKEN (Book #12)
SO CRUEL (Book #13)
SO HAUNTED (Book #14)
SO SILENT (Book #15)

SO BLEAK (Book #16)
SO HOLLOW (Book #17)

FIONA RED MYSTERY SERIES
LET HER GO (Book #1)
LET HER BE (Book #2)
LET HER HOPE (Book #3)
LET HER WISH (Book #4)
LET HER LIVE (Book #5)
LET HER RUN (Book #6)
LET HER HIDE (Book #7)
LET HER BELIEVE (Book #8)
LET HER FORGET (Book #9)
LET HER TRY (Book #10)
LET HER PLAY (Book #11)
LET HER VANISH (Book #12)
LET HER FADE (Book #13)

DAISY FORTUNE MYSTERY SERIES
NEED YOU (Book #1)
CLAIM YOU (Book #2)
CRAVE YOU (Book #3)
CHOOSE YOU (Book #4)
CHASE YOU (Book #5)

AMBER YOUNG MYSTERY SERIES
ABSENT PITY (Book #1)
ABSENT REMORSE (Book #2)
ABSENT FEELING (Book #3)
ABSENT MERCY (Book #4)
ABSENT REASON (Book #5)
ABSENT SANITY (Book #6)
ABSENT LIFE (Book #7)
ABSENT HUMANITY (Book #8)

CAMI LARK MYSTERY SERIES
JUST ME (Book #1)
JUST OUTSIDE (Book #2)
JUST RIGHT (Book #3)
JUST FORGET (Book #4)

JUST ONCE (Book #5)
JUST HIDE (Book #6)
JUST NOW (Book #7)
JUST HOPE (Book #8)
JUST LEAVE (Book #9)
JUST TONIGHT (Book #10)

NICKY LYONS MYSTERY SERIES
ALL MINE (Book #1)
ALL HIS (Book #2)
ALL HE SEES (Book #3)
ALL ALONE (Book #4)
ALL FOR ONE (Book #5)
ALL HE TAKES (Book #6)
ALL FOR ME (Book #7)
ALL IN (Book #8)

CORA SHIELDS MYSTERY SERIES
UNDONE (Book #1)
UNWANTED (Book #2)
UNHINGED (Book #3)
UNSAID (Book #4)
UNGLUED (Book #5)
UNSTABLE (Book #6)
UNKNOWN (Book #7)
UNAWARE (Book #8)

MAY MOORE SUSPENSE THRILLER
NEVER RUN (Book #1)
NEVER TELL (Book #2)
NEVER LIVE (Book #3)
NEVER HIDE (Book #4)
NEVER FORGIVE (Book #5)
NEVER AGAIN (Book #6)
NEVER LOOK BACK (Book #7)
NEVER FORGET (Book #8)
NEVER LET GO (Book #9)
NEVER PRETEND (Book #10)
NEVER HESITATE (Book #11)

PAIGE KING MYSTERY SERIES
THE GIRL HE PINED (Book #1)
THE GIRL HE CHOSE (Book #2)
THE GIRL HE TOOK (Book #3)
THE GIRL HE WISHED (Book #4)
THE GIRL HE CROWNED (Book #5)
THE GIRL HE WATCHED (Book #6)
THE GIRL HE WANTED (Book #7)
THE GIRL HE CLAIMED (Book #8)

VALERIE LAW MYSTERY SERIES
NO MERCY (Book #1)
NO PITY (Book #2)
NO FEAR (Book #3)
NO SLEEP (Book #4)
NO QUARTER (Book #5)
NO CHANCE (Book #6)
NO REFUGE (Book #7)
NO GRACE (Book #8)
NO ESCAPE (Book #9)

RACHEL GIFT MYSTERY SERIES
HER LAST WISH (Book #1)
HER LAST CHANCE (Book #2)
HER LAST HOPE (Book #3)
HER LAST FEAR (Book #4)
HER LAST CHOICE (Book #5)
HER LAST BREATH (Book #6)
HER LAST MISTAKE (Book #7)
HER LAST DESIRE (Book #8)
HER LAST REGRET (Book #9)
HER LAST HOUR (Book #10)
HER LAST SHOT (Book #11)
HER LAST PRAYER (Book #12)
HER LAST LIE (Book #13)
HER LAST WHISPER (Book #14)
HER LAST SECRET (Book #15)

AVA GOLD MYSTERY SERIES
CITY OF PREY (Book #1)

CITY OF FEAR (Book #2)
CITY OF BONES (Book #3)
CITY OF GHOSTS (Book #4)
CITY OF DEATH (Book #5)
CITY OF VICE (Book #6)

A YEAR IN EUROPE
A MURDER IN PARIS (Book #1)
DEATH IN FLORENCE (Book #2)
VENGEANCE IN VIENNA (Book #3)
A FATALITY IN SPAIN (Book #4)

ELLA DARK FBI SUSPENSE THRILLER
GIRL, ALONE (Book #1)
GIRL, TAKEN (Book #2)
GIRL, HUNTED (Book #3)
GIRL, SILENCED (Book #4)
GIRL, VANISHED (Book 5)
GIRL ERASED (Book #6)
GIRL, FORSAKEN (Book #7)
GIRL, TRAPPED (Book #8)
GIRL, EXPENDABLE (Book #9)
GIRL, ESCAPED (Book #10)
GIRL, HIS (Book #11)
GIRL, LURED (Book #12)
GIRL, MISSING (Book #13)
GIRL, UNKNOWN (Book #14)
GIRL, DECEIVED (Book #15)
GIRL, FORLORN (Book #16)
GIRL, REMADE (Book #17)
GIRL, BETRAYED (Book #18)
GIRL, BOUND (Book #19)
GIRL, REFORMED (Book #20)
GIRL, REBORN (Book #21)

LAURA FROST FBI SUSPENSE THRILLER
ALREADY GONE (Book #1)
ALREADY SEEN (Book #2)
ALREADY TRAPPED (Book #3)
ALREADY MISSING (Book #4)

ALREADY DEAD (Book #5)
ALREADY TAKEN (Book #6)
ALREADY CHOSEN (Book #7)
ALREADY LOST (Book #8)
ALREADY HIS (Book #9)
ALREADY LURED (Book #10)
ALREADY COLD (Book #11)

EUROPEAN VOYAGE COZY MYSTERY SERIES
MURDER (AND BAKLAVA) (Book #1)
DEATH (AND APPLE STRUDEL) (Book #2)
CRIME (AND LAGER) (Book #3)
MISFORTUNE (AND GOUDA) (Book #4)
CALAMITY (AND A DANISH) (Book #5)
MAYHEM (AND HERRING) (Book #6)

ADELE SHARP MYSTERY SERIES
LEFT TO DIE (Book #1)
LEFT TO RUN (Book #2)
LEFT TO HIDE (Book #3)
LEFT TO KILL (Book #4)
LEFT TO MURDER (Book #5)
LEFT TO ENVY (Book #6)
LEFT TO LAPSE (Book #7)
LEFT TO VANISH (Book #8)
LEFT TO HUNT (Book #9)
LEFT TO FEAR (Book #10)
LEFT TO PREY (Book #11)
LEFT TO LURE (Book #12)
LEFT TO CRAVE (Book #13)
LEFT TO LOATHE (Book #14)
LEFT TO HARM (Book #15)
LEFT TO RUIN (Book #16)

THE AU PAIR SERIES
ALMOST GONE (Book#1)
ALMOST LOST (Book #2)
ALMOST DEAD (Book #3)

ZOE PRIME MYSTERY SERIES

FACE OF DEATH (Book#1)
FACE OF MURDER (Book #2)
FACE OF FEAR (Book #3)
FACE OF MADNESS (Book #4)
FACE OF FURY (Book #5)
FACE OF DARKNESS (Book #6)

A JESSIE HUNT PSYCHOLOGICAL SUSPENSE SERIES
THE PERFECT WIFE (Book #1)
THE PERFECT BLOCK (Book #2)
THE PERFECT HOUSE (Book #3)
THE PERFECT SMILE (Book #4)
THE PERFECT LIE (Book #5)
THE PERFECT LOOK (Book #6)
THE PERFECT AFFAIR (Book #7)
THE PERFECT ALIBI (Book #8)
THE PERFECT NEIGHBOR (Book #9)
THE PERFECT DISGUISE (Book #10)
THE PERFECT SECRET (Book #11)
THE PERFECT FAÇADE (Book #12)
THE PERFECT IMPRESSION (Book #13)
THE PERFECT DECEIT (Book #14)
THE PERFECT MISTRESS (Book #15)
THE PERFECT IMAGE (Book #16)
THE PERFECT VEIL (Book #17)
THE PERFECT INDISCRETION (Book #18)
THE PERFECT RUMOR (Book #19)
THE PERFECT COUPLE (Book #20)
THE PERFECT MURDER (Book #21)
THE PERFECT HUSBAND (Book #22)
THE PERFECT SCANDAL (Book #23)
THE PERFECT MASK (Book #24)
THE PERFECT RUSE (Book #25)
THE PERFECT VENEER (Book #26)
THE PERFECT PEOPLE (Book #27)
THE PERFECT WITNESS (Book #28)
THE PERFECT APPEARANCE (Book #29)
THE PERFECT TRAP (Book #30)
THE PERFECT EXPRESSION (Book #31)
THE PERFECT ACCOMPLICE (Book #32)

THE PERFECT SHOW (Book #33)
THE PERFECT POISE (Book #34)
THE PERFECT CROWD (Book #35)
THE PERFECT CRIME (Book #36)
THE PERFECT PREY (Book #37)
THE PERFECT BETRAYAL (Book #38)

CHLOE FINE PSYCHOLOGICAL SUSPENSE SERIES
NEXT DOOR (Book #1)
A NEIGHBOR'S LIE (Book #2)
CUL DE SAC (Book #3)
SILENT NEIGHBOR (Book #4)
HOMECOMING (Book #5)
TINTED WINDOWS (Book #6)

KATE WISE MYSTERY SERIES
IF SHE KNEW (Book #1)
IF SHE SAW (Book #2)
IF SHE RAN (Book #3)
IF SHE HID (Book #4)
IF SHE FLED (Book #5)
IF SHE FEARED (Book #6)
IF SHE HEARD (Book #7)

THE MAKING OF RILEY PAIGE SERIES
WATCHING (Book #1)
WAITING (Book #2)
LURING (Book #3)
TAKING (Book #4)
STALKING (Book #5)
KILLING (Book #6)

RILEY PAIGE MYSTERY SERIES
ONCE GONE (Book #1)
ONCE TAKEN (Book #2)
ONCE CRAVED (Book #3)
ONCE LURED (Book #4)
ONCE HUNTED (Book #5)
ONCE PINED (Book #6)
ONCE FORSAKEN (Book #7)

ONCE COLD (Book #8)
ONCE STALKED (Book #9)
ONCE LOST (Book #10)
ONCE BURIED (Book #11)
ONCE BOUND (Book #12)
ONCE TRAPPED (Book #13)
ONCE DORMANT (Book #14)
ONCE SHUNNED (Book #15)
ONCE MISSED (Book #16)
ONCE CHOSEN (Book #17)

MACKENZIE WHITE MYSTERY SERIES
BEFORE HE KILLS (Book #1)
BEFORE HE SEES (Book #2)
BEFORE HE COVETS (Book #3)
BEFORE HE TAKES (Book #4)
BEFORE HE NEEDS (Book #5)
BEFORE HE FEELS (Book #6)
BEFORE HE SINS (Book #7)
BEFORE HE HUNTS (Book #8)
BEFORE HE PREYS (Book #9)
BEFORE HE LONGS (Book #10)
BEFORE HE LAPSES (Book #11)
BEFORE HE ENVIES (Book #12)
BEFORE HE STALKS (Book #13)
BEFORE HE HARMS (Book #14)

AVERY BLACK MYSTERY SERIES
CAUSE TO KILL (Book #1)
CAUSE TO RUN (Book #2)
CAUSE TO HIDE (Book #3)
CAUSE TO FEAR (Book #4)
CAUSE TO SAVE (Book #5)
CAUSE TO DREAD (Book #6)

KERI LOCKE MYSTERY SERIES
A TRACE OF DEATH (Book #1)
A TRACE OF MURDER (Book #2)
A TRACE OF VICE (Book #3)
A TRACE OF CRIME (Book #4)

A TRACE OF HOPE (Book #5)

PROLOGUE

The London fog was a living, breathing entity, a thick, palpable presence that enveloped the city like a shroud. It hung heavy in the air, muffling the usual sounds of the metropolis, turning the familiar streets into an eerie, otherworldly landscape. Emily Stanton navigated this surreal world with a mixture of excitement and trepidation; her phone held high to capture every unsettling detail for her ever-present online audience.

At twenty-four, Emily had built a life and a career on sharing her experiences with the world. Her followers were her constant companions, a digital entourage that accompanied her on every adventure, every foray into the unknown. Tonight, they were with her as she delved into the mysterious heart of nocturnal London, eager to experience the city's secrets through her eyes.

"Can you believe this fog?" she whispered into her phone, her voice tinged with a combination of awe and unease. The camera panned across the scene, capturing the way the mist curled around the old, worn buildings, transforming the ordinary into something sinister and unfamiliar. "It's like something out of a Victorian ghost story. I keep expecting to see Jack the Ripper lurking in the shadows, or maybe Dr. Jekyll prowling the streets in search of his next victim."

The comments flooded in, a cascading stream of thumbs up, heart emojis, and words of encouragement. Some of her followers urged her on, eager for more of the atmospheric footage, thrilled by the prospect of vicarious thrills. Others expressed concern for her safety, urging her to be careful, to watch her step in the treacherous fog. Emily smiled, drawing comfort from their digital presence. She wasn't alone out here in the mist – her followers were with her every step of the way.

As she rounded a corner, a shape loomed out of the fog ahead, stopping her dead in her tracks. It was a building, but not like the others she'd passed on her nighttime stroll. This one seemed to emanate a sense of history, of secrets long buried and forgotten. It was as if the structure itself was whispering to her, beckoning her to come closer, to uncover the mysteries that lay within its walls.

Intrigued, Emily zoomed in on the facade, trying to make out the details through the swirling fog. The building was old, that much was clear, with crumbling brickwork and boarded-up windows that spoke of long neglect. But there was something else, something that tugged at the edges of her mind, a nagging sense of familiarity that she couldn't quite place.

"Look at this, guys," she breathed, her voice hushed with excitement. "I'd heard it was here. It's an old, abandoned bathhouse. I've never seen anything like it before. I wonder what stories it could tell, what secrets it might hold..."

Her followers were quick to respond, some sharing her excitement, others urging caution. A few claimed to know the history of the place, spinning tales of dark deeds and restless spirits. They spoke of a Victorian-era bathhouse, once a place of relaxation and rejuvenation, now reduced to a crumbling ruin, haunted by the ghosts of its past. Emily felt a thrill run through her, a mix of fear and anticipation. This was the kind of moment she lived for – the chance to explore the unknown, to uncover the secrets that the city kept hidden. But all was not as it seemed. She herself was performing. She had prepared somewhat for the destination, unbeknownst to her viewers. It was not as happenstance as it appeared.

With a deep breath, she approached the bathhouse, her footsteps echoing loudly on the damp pavement. The building seemed to grow as she drew near, looming over her like a slumbering giant, waiting to be awakened. A part of her wanted to turn back, to retreat to the safety of the well-lit streets and the comforting glow of her phone screen. But she pushed the feeling aside, steeling herself for whatever lay ahead. She had a responsibility to her followers, to her own sense of adventure. She couldn't back down now, not when she was so close to discovering something truly extraordinary.

The door groaned as she pushed it open, the sound echoing through the cavernous space beyond. Emily stepped inside, her phone's light cutting through the gloom, casting eerie shadows on the crumbling walls. The interior of the bathhouse was a testament to neglect, a once-grand space now reduced to a shell of its former self. Cracked tiles, stained walls, and pools long since drained of water greeted her, a stark reminder of the passage of time and the inevitability of decay.

"I can't believe this place," she murmured, her voice sounding small and muffled in the vast room. "It's like something out of a dream... or a nightmare. I can almost feel the weight of the years pressing down on me."

She moved deeper into the bathhouse, her phone capturing every eerie detail, every haunting vignette. The comments continued to pour in, some of her followers sharing her sense of wonder, others growing increasingly worried for her well-being. Emily tried to reassure them, to laugh off their concerns, but she couldn't shake the growing sense of unease that gnawed at her stomach, the feeling that she was being watched by unseen eyes.

And then, in the periphery of her vision, a flicker of movement. A shadow, darting across the far wall, too fast to be a trick of the light. Emily spun around, her heart hammering in her chest, her breath coming in short, sharp gasps. The beam of her phone scanned the room, searching for the source of the disturbance, but there was nothing there. Just the empty, echoing space, and the relentless press of the darkness.

"It's okay, guys," she said, forcing a laugh that sounded hollow even to her own ears. "Just my imagination playing tricks on me. There's nothing to be scared of here. It's just an old, abandoned building, right?"

But even as the words left her mouth, she knew they weren't true. There was something in the bathhouse with her, something that didn't belong. She could feel it watching her, could sense its malevolent presence lurking just beyond the reach of her phone's light. It was as if the very walls were alive, pulsing with a dark, ancient energy that threatened to consume her.

She took a step back, ready to flee, to abandon this place and never look back. But it was too late. A figure emerged from the shadows, a specter clad in Victorian finery, its face hidden behind a grinning mask that leered at her with a twisted, mocking expression. Emily's scream caught in her throat, her phone tumbling from her suddenly numb fingers as she stared at the apparition in mute horror.

The figure loomed over her, a disjointed poem spilling from its lips, a hymn of madness and despair that echoed through the cavernous space.

"Dark, the time in which we live. No peace, not life, we shan't forgive. For those who fame above all crave shall lie within an unmarked grave."

Emily tried to run, to push past the specter and escape into the night, but her legs wouldn't obey, rooted to the spot by a terror deeper than any she'd ever known. The last thing she saw, before the darkness

3

claimed her, was the glint of a blade in the figure's hand, and the endless, pitiless gaze of the mask, staring into her soul.

Her phone lay forgotten on the cracked tile, a mute witness to the horror that had unfolded. On its screen, the comments continued to scroll by, a litany of confusion and growing dread as her followers tried to make sense of what they'd just seen. And then, abruptly, the feed cut out, leaving only a final, chilling image – the masked figure, bending down to stare directly into the camera, its eyes glittering with a madness born of ages past.

In the silence that followed, the fog seemed to thicken, swallowing the bathhouse and the secrets it held. The city slumbered on, unaware of the horror that had just taken place in its midst. And somewhere in the depths of the mist, a figure in Victorian garb slipped away, melting into the shadows like a ghost, leaving only a trail of whispered poems and the memory of a scream in its wake.

CHAPTER ONE

Finn Wright felt a familiar sense of unease as he and Amelia Winters approached Rob's aunt's cottage in the quiet village of Great Amwell. The peaceful surroundings, with their quaint houses and well-tended gardens, stood in stark contrast to the purpose of their visit. Max Vilne, the killer who had haunted Finn's thoughts for far too long, had been sighted in the area, and Finn was determined to bring him to justice once and for all.

As they pulled up to the cottage, Finn saw that the police were already on the scene, their cars parked haphazardly on the narrow lane. He exchanged a glance with Amelia, seeing his own determination mirrored in her eyes. They were a team, a partnership forged in the heat of countless investigations, and he drew strength from her presence.

Rob greeted them as they exited the car, his usually cheerful face creased with worry. "Finn, Amelia, thanks for coming so quickly," he said, shaking their hands. "We've been searching the area, but so far, no sign of Vilne."

Finn nodded, his jaw clenching with frustration. Vilne had proven to be a slippery target, always one step ahead of the law. But Finn refused to let him slip away again. "What about the sightings?" he asked, his voice tense. "Are they credible?"

Rob sighed, running a hand through his hair. "They seem to be. Several people reported seeing a man matching Vilne's description in the village yesterday. We're taking it very seriously, but you know how elusive he can be."

Finn felt a surge of anger mixed with a hint of guilt. Vilne was his responsibility, his failure. He should have caught him long ago before more innocent lives were lost. "We'll find him," he said, his voice low and intense. "We have to."

"Is it your fault he escaped after you caught him in the US? While you were here in England?" Amelia asked with a raised eyebrow. "Is it your fault he pulled strings to put you under pressure, manipulated people, then smuggled himself to the UK to have revenge on you? All because you had the audacity to catch him in the first place?"

"Well, when you put it like that..." Finn grinned. He loved that Amelia always tried to build people up.

Amelia laid a hand on his arm, her touch a gentle reminder of her support. "We will catch him," she said, her voice filled with quiet confidence. "But first, let's take a look around, see if we can find any clues. Last time he tried to threaten you, he left something, remember?"

Finn nodded, grateful for her level-headedness. Together, they set off to search the cottage grounds, their eyes scanning the surroundings for any signs of disturbance. As they walked, they fell into their familiar rhythm, discussing the case and bouncing ideas off each other.

"I just don't understand," Finn said, his brow furrowed. "Why would Vilne come here, of all places? Surely he knew we were watching after the incident when he broke in months ago? What's his game?"

Amelia shook her head, her red hair glinting in the sunlight. "I don't know. Maybe he wanted to show you he could. But he's always had a reason for his actions, twisted as they may be. We just need to figure out what it is this time."

Just as Finn was about to suggest they regroup with Rob, something caught his eye. There, in a tree on a distant hill, something was hanging from the branches.

"Amelia, look," he said, pointing. "What do you make of that?"

She squinted, shielding her eyes from the sun. "It's hard to tell from here. Could be some kind of local tradition or prank. But I think we should check it out."

Finn agreed, and they set off towards the hill, their steps quickening with a sense of purpose. As they walked, Finn found himself reflecting on their partnership, on the trust and affection that had grown between them over the last year. Amelia was more than just a colleague; she was his rock, his anchor in the turbulent world of criminal investigation. He could have fallen apart waiting for his court case in the US, but everything Rob and Amelia had done for him, giving him purpose as a consultant detective, had saved them.

He would do anything to return the favor.

As they neared the tree, the hanging objects came into clearer view, and Finn felt a chill run down his spine. They were mannequins, three of them swaying gently in the breeze. Even from a distance, he could tell that this was no prank or tradition. This had Vilne's sinister touch all over it.

Amelia's sharp intake of breath told him she had come to the same conclusion. They exchanged a look, a silent communication born of years of working together, and quickened their pace.

When they reached the tree, Finn's worst fears were confirmed. Each mannequin bore a name, written in bold, black letters: "Finn," "Amelia," "Rob." It was a message, a taunt from Vilne, making it clear that he was targeting not just Finn, but those closest to him.

Finn felt a rush of anger, his hands clenching into fists at his sides. Vilne was playing with them, toying with their lives like a cat with a mouse. But Finn refused to be a pawn in his sick game. He would find Vilne, and he would make him pay for every life he had destroyed.

Amelia's hand on his shoulder brought him back to the present. He looked down at her, seeing the same fierce determination in her eyes that he felt in his own heart. "He's desperate doing something like this," she said, her voice low and intense. "He wanted to hurt you by abducting Demi, but we saved her and now she's safe back in the States. Now, he's angry. He's trying to frighten us, but I think he's the frightened one. We'll catch him..."

He nodded, drawing strength from her words, from the unwavering support he saw in her gaze. "Together," he echoed, his voice a promise.

Just as they were about to turn around, Finn spotted something at the foot of the tree, wedged inside a hole in the trunk.

"What's that?" Finn asked out loud.

"It looks metallic," Amelia said.

Finn leaned down and poked his finger inside. With a little effort, the object popped out. It was an old pocket watch made of brass. Finn flipped it around to see no description.

"Looks old," Amelia said. "It's possible it's been there for some time."

"Maybe," Finn said, looking around.

They made their way back down the hill, the weight of their discovery heavy on their shoulders. Rob was waiting for them, his face etched with concern. When they told him about the mannequins, his eyes widened with shock and anger.

"That scumbag," he muttered, shaking his head. "He's taunting us, trying to get under our skin."

Finn nodded grimly. "And it's working. But we can't let him dictate the terms of this game. We need to stay focused, stay one step ahead."

"Agreed," Rob said. "I promise we'll increase security around the cottage and put out an alert for Vilne."

7

Finn felt a surge of gratitude for his friend's support, mixed with a twinge of guilt for putting him in danger. But as Amelia had said, Vilne was the only one to blame. And they would stop him, no matter the cost.

Just as they were about to head back to the cottage to regroup, Amelia's phone rang. She answered, her face growing grave as she listened to the caller. When she hung up, she turned to Finn, her expression somber.

"Are you sure?" she said. "I understand. We'll be right there." The call ended.

"What's wrong?" asked Finn.

"There's a murder higher-ups want us to take a look at," she said, her voice tight. "A body found in an abandoned Victorian bathhouse. The scene is...disturbing. They are worried it's Vilne because of the theatricality of it."

Finn felt a chill run through him, a sense of foreboding that he couldn't shake. "Vilne?" he asked, though he already knew the answer.

Amelia nodded. "Nothing would surprise me. We need to get there, see if we can find out if it's really him. If not, the Home Office wants us to investigate anyway. Apparently it involved an influencer, and her death has caused a panic on social media."

"Usually the Home Office contact me first," Rob said.

"Don't feel left out, Chief," Amelia said. "If you want, I could pretend they didn't call and you can go over it all again, like you're sending your trusted duo out there to catch a killer."

Rob laughed. "Amelia, you're spending too much time with Finn. He's usually the one making snarky jokes."

"I resent that," Finn said.

"Good," Rob said, patting him on the back. "But please. Be careful, you two. We can't afford to let our guard down for one second. I can't help but feel Vilne is leading us into a trap."

Finn agreed, his mind already racing with possibilities. He knew they were heading into something dark and dangerous, but he also knew that with Amelia by his side, he could face anything.

"Keep me abridged," Rob said, walking off to speak with a constable nearby."

As Finn and Amelia climbed into the car, Finn took one last look at the ominous mannequins hanging from the tree. They seemed to stare back at him, their blank faces a mocking reminder of the evil they were up against. But Finn refused to be intimidated. He had a job to do, a

8

killer to catch. And he wouldn't rest until Max Vilne was behind bars and the world was a little bit safer.

"Winters," Finn said. "You mentioned a Victorian Bathhouse?"

"Yes, where the body was found."

"That watch up on the hill," Finn mused out loud. "I wonder if it was Victorian, too."

"It was old, but it might have nothing to do with Vilne or this case," Amelia said. "It's possibly been a coincidence."

"Or a cryptic warning of what's to come from Vilne."

With a grim sense of determination, Finn started the engine, ready to confront whatever horrors awaited them at the bathhouse. The game was on, and more than ever, Finn was determined to win.

CHAPTER TWO

As Finn stepped out of the car, the abandoned Victorian bathhouse loomed before him, a crumbling monument to a bygone era. Beside him, Amelia Winters surveyed the scene, her keen eyes taking in every detail. "I don't like the look of this place," she murmured, her voice low and troubled. "There's something about it that feels... wrong."

Finn nodded, feeling a chill run down his spine despite the warmth of the day. "You're frightened of buildings, now?"

"Don't start," Amelia said before affecting an American accent. "We can't all be 'mister American tough guy, taking on the world's evils, one bad guy at a time'."

"I understand," Finn smiled. "It must be difficult for you being around such a powerfully handsome individual. But please, hands off. Not during an investigation."

Amelia shook her head, but he could see the glint of playfulness in her eyes.

They ducked under the police cordon and made their way towards the entrance, the gravel crunching beneath their feet.

Detective Inspector Grayson, a seasoned officer with a grim demeanor, greeted them with a curt nod. "Finn, Inspector Winters. Glad you could make it out so quickly."

Finn shook his hand, noting the tight lines around the inspector's eyes. "Of course. What have we got?"

Grayson sighed, his gaze flickering towards the bathhouse. "It's a nasty one. Victim is Emily Stanton, a young socialite and influencer. Found dead in the main bathing chamber while live streaming, posed like some sort of museum display. The whole scene has this eerie Victorian vibe. Straight out of Jack the Ripper's playbook."

Amelia frowned, her brow furrowing. "Victorian? That's an odd choice for a murder scene."

"Odd is putting it mildly," Grayson said, shaking his head. "It's like something out of a penny dreadful. But I'll let you see for yourselves."

As they entered the bathhouse, Finn couldn't suppress the shudder that ran through him. The air inside was thick and heavy, laden with the weight of history and decay. The dimly lit corridors stretched out before them, the sound of dripping water and creaking floorboards echoing in the stillness.

"It's incredible to me that places like this still exist," Finn whispered, his voice hushed in the oppressive atmosphere. Even after all that time, the history of the UK fascinated him. Sometimes, it felt as though in every direction, you just had to walk for a few minutes to find something Victorian or older.

"It gives me the creeps," Amelia said. "I wish places like this could explain what happened within their walls."

Finn nodded. "And whatever it's trying to tell us, I doubt it's anything good."

When they reached the main bathing chamber, the sight that greeted them was like something out of a nightmare. Emily's body lay in the center of the room, surrounded by flickering candles and withered rose petals. She was dressed in a Victorian-style gown, her blonde hair arranged in elaborate curls. At first glance, she could have been mistaken for a sleeping princess from a fairy tale, but the illusion was shattered by the unnatural pallor of her skin, the vicious stab wounds on her milky skin, and the dark bruises around her neck.

Amelia approached the body, her steps careful and measured. She knelt down, her gloved fingers gently brushing against Emily's wrist. "Her smartwatch is still blinking," she said, her voice tinged with disbelief. "It's such a jarring contrast, this modern piece of technology against all this Victorian decor."

Finn joined her, his eyes scanning the room for any clues the killer might have left behind. "It's like two worlds colliding," he mused, his gaze lingering on the ornate tiles and the intricate metalwork. "The past and the present. We shouldn't rule out the connection as a possible motive."

"If Emily was live streaming," Amelia said, rising to her feet. "Perhaps the killer was wanting to stop silence her from revealing something?"

Finn nodded, his expression grim. "It's possible, but I've seen live streamers being murdered while recording before. It could be that the killer was watching the stream and decided to come here."

"I don't know," Amelia sighed. "The candle, the rose petals, that doesn't sound like a spontaneous act."

"He could be a killer who was waiting for an opportunity," Finn replied. "Then, he sees Emily streaming and grabs the things he had already prepared for his first kill."

As they searched the room, a glint of something caught Finn's eye. He knelt down, his fingers brushing against a loose tile. With a gentle tug, the tile came free, revealing a small, leather-bound book nestled in the dust.

"What have you got there?" Amelia asked, joining him.

Finn held up the book, his eyes widening as he flipped through the pages. "Strange… Seems like it's someone's notebook. It's filled with notes and sketches about the bathhouse, about its history. And look at this..." He pointed to the final entry, dated just two days prior. "It mentions a secret chamber hidden somewhere in the building. The question is, was this Emily's, the killer's, or someone else's?"

"If it's the killer's," Amelia mused out loud, "then he could have been here already and Emily was in the wrong place at the wrong time."

Finn's eyes lit up, looking at the notebook. "A secret chamber, though…"

Amelia's eyes sparkled with excitement, despite the grim circumstances. "A hidden room? That could have been where the killer was hiding."

"Exactly," Finn said, rising to his feet. "If our killer is as obsessed with the Victorian era as they seem to be, they might have used this secret chamber for something. Maybe it's where they planned all of this."

Amelia's face grew serious. "Or maybe it's where they're keeping their next victim."

A chill ran down Finn's spine at the thought. "Let's look for anything out of place. A hatch on a floor or a wall that seems out of place."

But before they could explore the lead further, a commotion from outside drew their attention. They emerged from the bathhouse to find a young man arguing with the officers at the cordon, his face etched with grief and desperation.

Finn approached him, his hands held up in a calming gesture. "Hey, easy there. I'm consulting detective Finn Wright, and this is my partner, Inspector Amelia Winters. We're investigating Emily's murder. Are you a friend of hers?"

The man's eyes, red-rimmed and haunted, met Finn's. "I'm Liam Holden… I'm Emily's boyfriend. Or I was, I guess." His voice broke, a sob catching in his throat. "I can't believe she's gone. I can't believe someone would do this to her."

Amelia stepped forward, her voice gentle. "We're so sorry for your loss, Liam. I know this is a difficult time, but anything you can tell us about Emily, about her life, could help us find who did this."

The boyfriend nodded, his hands clenching and unclenching at his sides. "She was... she was amazing. So full of life, so passionate about everything she did. She loved streaming for her fans. But lately, she'd been getting these messages. Threats. Emily thought it went with the territory as her profile became more popular, but I told her to be careful."

Finn's brow furrowed. "Were any of these threats specific? What did they say?"

"She'd receive the usual unsolicited pictures from men every now and then," Liam explained, "and the usual troll comments. But things changed a few weeks back."

"Changed, how?" Amelia asked.

"Some of the threats were weird. Something about her being too obsessed with social media, with technology. The messages said she needed to disconnect, to break free. At first, she just laughed them off, said it was probably just some troll trying to get a rise out of her. But they kept coming, getting more and more intense."

"Did the messages say anything specific?" Amelia asked, her pen poised over her notebook. "Any clues about who might have sent them or why they were targeting Emily?"

The boyfriend shook his head. "No, nothing like that. But..." He hesitated, his eyes flickering between Finn and Amelia. "There was something else. Something Emily said a few days ago."

Finn leaned in, his heart pounding. "What was it?"

"She said she'd found something. Something about the bathhouse, about its history. She was excited about it, said it was going to be a big story. But she wouldn't tell me what it was. Said she needed to verify some things first."

"So she chose here, tonight?" Finn asked.

Liam nodded. "But she sometimes pretended on her live streams to just happen to find a place, or that it was her first time there."

"To create a sense of adventure for those watching," Finn said, nodding.

"That's right," Liam said, wiping tears from his eyes.

Amelia exchanged a glance with Finn, a flicker of understanding passing between them. "It's possible then that Emily had been here before, to scout out the place?"

"Yes," Liam said. "But she had stopped sharing with me where she was going on live streams because she thought I was being overly protective... Now look what happened..."

Finn had heard that line before. One partner's "over protection" could be another partner's controlling abuse.

"Was Emily scared of you?" Finn asked.

"What!?" Liam said, loudly. "No! Of course not!"

"If she didn't want to share things with you because you were being too controlling," Finn went on, "could she have been worried about what you might do to her, if she went against your wishes?"

Liam shook his head. "You police are all the same... No... I loved her. I was only concerned, and it had been the source of some tension. Emily decided to draw a line between her professional and personal life."

"But you didn't like that..." Finn pressed.

"No," Liam said, now more calm. "But I respected her decision and left it alone. You can't tell your partner what to do, you can only give them advice."

"Did Emily tell anyone else about the threats? Her friends, her family?" Amelia's pen remained poised over her notebook.

The boyfriend shook his head. "No, she... she didn't want to worry anyone. She said she could handle it, that it wasn't a big deal. That every creative has to put up with that these days." A tear slipped down his cheek, glistening in the sunlight. "I should have pushed harder. I should have made her go to the police. Maybe if I had..."

Finn laid a hand on the man's shoulder, his grip firm and reassuring. "Hey, this is not your fault. The only person to blame is the one who did this to Emily. And I promise you, we're going to find them."

"Thank you," Liam nodded.

"Liam," Amelia said pointing to Detective Grayson, who was standing nearby with two constables, going over their notes. "Could you give your statement to the detective over there?"

Finn waved at Inspector Grayson, who nodded in return and walked Liam slowly away.

Amelia's eyes gleamed with determination as she turned to Finn, her voice low but resolute. "We need to go back inside, Finn. If there's a secret room hidden in this bathhouse, it might be where the killer was waiting for Emily."

Finn nodded in agreement, a sense of urgency creeping into his movements as they retraced their steps back into the dimly lit interior.

14

The air inside the bathhouse felt heavy with history and secrets, the flickering light casting eerie shadows on the tiled walls. Finn's footsteps echoed softly against the ancient floors as they moved cautiously through the corridors, their eyes scanning for any sign of an anomaly. The notebook clutched tightly in Finn's hand seemed to whisper of hidden passages and clandestine meetings, adding to the suspense that hung thick in the air. As they reached the spot where Emily's body had been found, Finn felt the coldness of the place, a silent reminder of the danger that lurked within those walls. Together, he and Amelia began to search for any subtle hint that could lead them to the elusive secret chamber mentioned in the notebook.

"Anything in there that could help?" Amelia said, pointing to the notebook in Finn's hands.

Finn opened it up and flicked through the pages. "There's a sketch here, looks like this hallway here , book ended by two rooms.

Finn's keen eyes scanned the area, his gaze lingering on the unusually thick wall separating the two rooms.

"Hmm," Finn said, rubbing his cheek.

"What is it?" Amelia asked.

"Doesn't this wall look a good bit longer than the two rooms?" Finn asked. "There's something not right about that."

His fingers traced along the wall until they found a small latch hidden in the intricate Victorian wallpaper. With a soft click, a section of the wall swung open, revealing a narrow passage leading into darkness.

"Open sesame," Finn said in a booming voice.

Amelia followed closely behind Finn as they stepped into the hidden room. Dust swirled in the air, settling on forgotten cobwebs that adorned the corners. Finn's disappointment was palpable as he surveyed the empty space, devoid of any clues or evidence.

"Well, this is disappointing," Finn muttered under his breath, his frustration evident in his tone. His nostrils stung slightly.

Amelia's brow furrowed as she observed their surroundings. "I'll get forensics to go over this place, but..." She paused, wrinkling her nose at a faint smell lingering in the air. "It stinks of bleach. It's like someone went to great lengths to clean this room out."

Finn's jaw clenched at the realization. "Deliberately cleaning it out suggests they were covering their tracks," he mused aloud, his mind already racing through possible scenarios. "This has got Max Vilne written all over it. Sometimes he liked to sterilize the scene to show his control over the investigating officers. If something is left behind, it's deliberate."

"We shouldn't jump to conclusions," Amelia reminded Finn. "If we see Vilne in all of this, we could miss the real killer."

"Come on, Winters," Finn said. "He's already threatened us again with those mannequins tied to the tree back at the cottage. Then there was that watch, probably Victorian-era like the bath house. He's showing us flashes of what he has in store."

Amelia didn't say anything, but Finn could tell she didn't quite buy it.

The dim light filtering through a cracked window cast eerie shadows across the bare walls of the secret chamber. Finn and Amelia exchanged a knowing look, both detectives recognizing that this empty room held secrets that had been meticulously erased by someone with something to hide.

"Forensics is still outside," Amelia said as they left the room. "I'll…"

Finn's phone buzzed in his pocket. He pulled it out, frowning at the unknown number on the screen. When he opened the message, his blood ran cold.

"What the hell," Finn said, trying to make sense of the message.

"What is it?"

"Amelia, look at this." He held out the phone, showing her the screen. "It asks 'are you enjoying the bathhouse?' followed by a poem:

'By kings and things of progress delight,
thy tide will poison thine own crimson night.'"

"What are those numbers at the end of the message?" Amelia asked.

"Looks like coordinates," Finn said.

Amelia opened her phone and punched in the coordinates to her maps app.

Amelia's eyes widened, a flicker of recognition crossing her face. "Those coordinates... they're for an old textile mill about a twenty minute drive from here. Let's see if we can get a trace on the number and then head there."

Finn nodded, his jaw clenching. "If this is from the killer, it looks like he is playing games with us. Sending us on some kind of twisted scavenger hunt."

Amelia looked at Finn, worry in her eyes like wells of deep unease. "But what will be found there?"

CHAPTER THREE

Finn killed the engine, and the old police car's rattle gave way to a silence that seemed to seep from the skeletal remains of the textile mill. He eyed the behemoth structure; it was a carcass of bricks and broken windows. The place had a weight to it, the weight of discarded history. A relic that time forgot, but crime did not.

Amelia's phone pinged. "No dice on the phone number," she said. "Looks like the number has been spoofed somehow."

"Looks like we got here first. Why do our cases always take us to the worst places?" Finn remarked dryly, stepping out into the crisp air. His breath formed clouds as he spoke. "The killer is a terrible tour guide, if that's his intention."

"England isn't all murder and detective stories," Amelia added, shutting her door with a thud that echoed off the desolate walls around them. She pulled her coat tighter around herself, as if the chill in the air was something foul that could be kept at bay.

"Should we wait for the forensics team and backup?" Finn asked.

"No," said Winters. "For all we know there's a victim in there that needs our help."

They approached the looming doorway, their steps careful on the gravel, each crunch beneath their feet punctuating the stillness. As they drew closer, Finn's eyes caught the dark outline of something unnatural on the door—a symbol that didn't belong.

"Midnight," Amelia murmured, her voice barely above a whisper as she traced the outline of the Victorian-style clock face spray-painted across the rusted metal door. The hands were stark, pointing straight up as though accusing the night sky. "The witching hour."

"Midnight is often used to represent the end times. Could be religious?" Finn questioned, raising an eyebrow as he studied the symbol.

"Common motif," she replied, her gaze not leaving the symbol. "It signifies a time when the veil between this world and the next is thinnest. When spirits are supposed to have more power."

"Let's hope we're dealing with just a flesh-and-blood killer," Finn said, reaching out to the door. "I had enough of ghosts on Huldra Island."

"Don't remind me," Amelia said.

Finn shook the thought. Several cases prior, he and Amelia had been caught in the mother of all storms on a remote Scottish island. He still wasn't sure if something he had seen that night was otherworldly or not, but the old abandoned mill in front of him now gave him a similar feeling of uncertainty.

Regardless, it was time to put on a brave face as always. "Shall we go to the dance?" Finn grinned.

"Lead the way, Detective Wright," Amelia answered, playing along with the pretense

Finn pushed against the door with the heel of his palm, feeling the resistance of time-worn hinges before it swung open with a groan. They stepped over the threshold together, their senses immediately assaulted by the mustiness of decay and the scent of secrets long buried under dust and neglect.

"Time to see what our host has prepared for us," Finn muttered, his hand instinctively resting where his weapon should have been. But this was the UK, and neither he nor Amelia were allowed to carry firearms.

The darkness inside seemed to swallow the light from outside, inviting them further into its depths.

"If we're lucky, this will just be a wild goose chase," Amelia said, her flashlight piercing the shadows as they moved forward, the beam bouncing off ancient machinery and piles of debris.

"Hopefully," Finn concluded, but his mind was already sifting through the possible outcomes of this macabre invitation.

Their footfalls echoed in the cavernous space, a rhythm set to the tempo of suspense. The beam of Finn's flashlight danced across the walls, revealing the skeletal remains of a once-thriving office. Desks stood like tombstones in the gloom, surfaces shrouded in dust as if preserving the last moments of activity before the mill's heart had stopped beating.

"Check this out," Amelia called from the far end of the room, her voice low and steady.

Finn navigated through the maze of furniture, his eyes adjusting to the dimness that clung to every corner. The cluttered desk in front of Amelia was a patchwork of yellowed paper and faded ink. He leaned in closer, squinting at the article clippings that lay scattered like pieces of a jigsaw begging to be solved. They varied in their origins. Books, newspapers, magazines; they all were discussing one subject matter—advances in technology over the last forty years.

"Did the killer leave these here or did someone else?" he murmured, thumbing through the articles, each one a litany of questions with no answers.

"Look at this." Amelia pointed to a scrap of paper half-buried beneath the clippings. Scrawled handwriting beckoned them with a riddle that sent a shiver down Finn's spine: "Time fades like a sun of old, and the killing stroke is fierce and bold."

"Why do we always get the literary ones?" Finn said, the note's implications twisting in his mind. "That's two poetic samples dealing with the passage of time."

"I doubt the killer sent us here for an English literature lesson," Amelia replied, her brow furrowed in thought. "Come on."

They continued deeper into the mill, the oppressive atmosphere gripping their nerves, tightly. The heavy air seemed to grow colder as they reached the machine room, where the mechanical and rusted remnants of industry still lingered.

But something was out of place.

There, in the center of the room, sat an old spinning jenny, its spindles reaching out like the limbs of a metal arachnid. However, it was not the rusted contraption that stole Finn's breath—it was the figure seated at it.

"Jesus," Finn exhaled, taking in the sight of a man in his thirties. Bound to the machine, lifeless eyes staring into nothingness, he made a grotesque monument to the decay all around. His body still looked fresh to Finn's eyes. "I wonder if the killer came here straight from the bathhouse or vice versa. By the look of the body, the two victims died within a few hours of each other."

"Poor guy... This is sick," Amelia said. "Watch your back. It feels like we're not alone."

A Victorian pocket watch protruded obscenely from his mouth, its golden surface smeared with dark stains.

"I knew it!" Finn said, pointing at the watch. "Now, do you doubt me? Another watch!"

"The watch in the tree looked like it might have been there for a while," Amelia said. "It could be a coincidence."

"Look at what it's set to," Finn said, gravely.

"Midnight..." Amelia whispered, the connection dawning on her. "Just like the image on the door of the mill. The witching hour."

"The killer has a message," Finn observed, staring at the morbidly pale face of the dead man before him.

"But what is it?" she agreed, circling the body with professional detachment, though her hand trembled ever so slightly. "He seems preoccupied with time."

Something moved in an unseen, shadowy corner. Finn spun around and caught the tale of a rat in his flashlight beam, scuttling away, deeper into the old mill.

"Let's get forensics in here," Finn said, the tension tight around his neck.

"If there's anything to find," Amelia explained. "The secret room at the bathhouse was wiped with bleach. I doubt the killer has left anything here to be found. He's careful."

Amelia moved the beam of her torch around the room and took a few steps away from the body. Suddenly, she stopped.

"What's this?"

Finn stepped forward, put on some forensic gloves and then crouched by a leather-bound book on the floor, its cover worn and edges softened by time. He flipped it open with a careful finger, dust motes swirling in the sparse light filtering through the mill's broken windows. Amelia leaned over his shoulder, her flashlight beam cutting a swath across the yellowed pages.

"Looks just like the one from the bathhouse," Amelia murmured, taking the book in hand from Finn and scanning the neat script that filled the pages.

"Any more secret rooms?" Finn asked.

"No. But we have a name for our victim," Amelia said, showing a page.

Finn peered at it in the dim light. "His name is Lucas Henshaw," the text read. "And he died like the others will die. The madness will end. The stroke of midnight is coming."

"There are some sketches of cogs or gears here," Amelia said. "They look like the pieces of a large machine. I've never seen anything like it."

"I wonder what it does," Finn said, tracing the lines of text that spoke of a man caught between two eras. "These gears look almost like a clock."

The cautious march of footsteps sounded, echoing throughout the rusted building. Finn looked at Amelia nervously and picked up a piece of metal from the ground. He instinctively stood in front of Amelia.

Soon, the ghostly white figures of the forensics team appeared. "You got here first," one of the men said, as if disappointed. "Is that for us?" He pointed to the piece of metal in Finn's hands.

"No, of course not," Finn answered, trying to avoid the embarrassment.

"We found a body," Amelia said, pointing to the corpse attached to the old spinning wheel.

The forensic team buzzed around them, their white suits ghostly figures against the backdrop of rusting iron and wood. One of the techs called them over, gesturing towards Henshaw's body. Finn and Amelia stood and watched, breathing in the musty air of the mill. Soon, the forensics team had finished their preliminary work.

"Blunt force trauma to the head," the one of them reported, pointing to the wound hidden beneath the man's dark hair. "Killer used something heavy with an indentation in it. Something from here, maybe."

Finn looked around, studying the environment. The place was littered with the rusted remains of a once vibrant mill.

Amelia picked her way through the debris on the floor, examining each piece of metal and wood as if it could whisper its secrets. She paused by a hefty gear, its teeth jagged and menacing. "This," she said, not touching it but hovering her hand above its surface.

"Let's get it bagged and tagged," Finn instructed, knowing that every moment they spent theorizing was another moment the killer was out there, planning the next move. "That gear looks similar to the sketches in the journal. It looks old, like it's discolored with copper oxidization"

"I think I see some bone fragments on it," Amelia pondered aloud, stepping back as the forensic team moved in.

"Seems so," Finn agreed, his eyes scanning the mill once more. "Well, we have two leads now. Our victim here, Luc Henshaw, and I think it might be worth going over more details with Emily Stanton's boyfriend."

"I agree," Emily said.

"Which trail of breadcrumbs do we follow first?" Finn asked in expectation.

There was some movement among the forensics team as one of them walked slowly over to Finn and Amelia.

"What is it?" Amelia asked.

"We found this in the victim's inside pocket," the man said, holding up a bloodied piece of paper in his blue-gloved hand.

Finn shone his flashlight on it. "Pendegrast's Curiosities. It's a handwritten receipt for something, but the blood has obscured most of the writing."

Amelia took out her phone and gazed at it while prodding in some information. "It's a shop in Torley Town. It's not far." Amelia grinned.

"Well," Finn said. "Make that three trails of breadcrumbs then."

Amelia looked at her watch. "If we're fast, we might catch them before closing."

"I'm game if you are," Finn offered.

Amelia turned towards the exit. "Let's find out what Luc Henshaw was buying before he died."

CHAPTER FOUR

Finn tapped the steering wheel rhythmically as they pulled up outside a cluttered antique shop, its windows filled with an assortment of bric-a-brac from another era. The sign above the door read 'Pendergast's Curiosities,' letters curling with faux nostalgia.

"Lucas Henshaw's last known purchase was from here," Amelia said, unfolding a piece of paper with the list of artifacts. "If only these objects could talk..."

"Winters, if you start telling me you're having conversations with objects," Finn replied, his gaze sharp as he surveyed the street before getting out of the car, "I may have to call the men in white coats."

"If I get committed before you, then it *must* be the end times," Amelia replied.

Stopping outside of the shop, Finn peered in through the window. He could see various pieces of antiques staring back at him like an old Jules Verne story. Antiques, old places, and history had always fascinated him since he was a kid. It was part of what thrilled him about the cases in the UK. There was always ancient history nearby, adding something different to the mix.

"This place looks great!" he said excitedly.

Amelia touched his arm. "Murder investigation first, wasting money later."

Finn nodded. "But I am definitely coming back here."

"I don't doubt it."

The bell above the antique shop door jingled discordantly as they entered. The air was thick with the scent of aged wood and metal polish. A man in his late sixties, wearing a waistcoat that had seen better days, peered at them through round spectacles perched precariously on his nose. His eyes held a flicker of recognition.

"Arthur Pendergast?" Finn asked.

"Indeed," the old man answered, his voice carrying the gravel of years passed. "And to what do I owe the pleasure of this visit?"

"Detective Wright, and this is Inspector Winters with the Home Office," Finn introduced, flashing his new consulting detective badge.

"Oh my," the man said, seeming somewhat flustered. "How can I help you? I… I assure you I do not deal in stolen goods."

"I'm sure you don't," Amelia said. "But we were hoping you could tell us about this receipt." Amelia held up the receipt, which was now housed in a clear piece of plastic.

"Is that blood?" Pendergast said with a gasp.

"I'm afraid so," answered Finn.

Amelia handed the receipt to the man. "Do you remember any of this? It was found on the body of a man we believe to be Lucas Henshaw,"

"Oh no! That's just terrible!" Pendergast said, shaking his head in disbelief. "I knew Mr Henshaw somewhat. He bought a few things from me over the years. I'm so sad to hear this. How did it happen?"

"What can you tell us about him?" Amelia asked, moving straight into her questions.

"He was a businessman, but that's about as much as I know. He was always quite pleasant to deal with," Pendergast mused, leaning back against a counter laden with pocket watches and compasses. "He had quite the eye for the eclectic, if I remember rightly. Interested in Victorian and pre-Victorian pieces."

Amelia stepped forward, her presence commanding yet respectful. "Mr. Pendergast, what did he buy from you the last time he was here?"

"Ah, yes, the difference engine," Pendergast said, his eyes alight with scholarly enthusiasm. "A remarkable piece, one of Babbage's finest concepts. It's a shame it was never fully realized in his time."

"Charles Babbage? Wasn't he the inventor of the modern computer?" Finn pressed, his mind connecting potential dots behind a steady gaze.

"Yes," Pendergast answered. "He built several prototypes for mechanical computers during the 1800s. But most were never completed. I was lucky to have a segment of one such prototype called a difference engine."

"What is a difference engine?" Finn asked.

"Like you said," Pendergast explained. "It's a rudimentary mechanical computer used for mathematical calculations. Fascinating to think about."

"And Lucas Henshaw bought that?" Amelia asked.

"Quite. He fancied himself a bit of a historian. Said something about the parallels between the technological revolutions of then and now. He was quite a rich man, very successful in the business world.

But history seemed to be his passion. " Pendergast's hands danced with a collector's passion. "The past informing the future and all that."

"Did he mention anything specific? Any project or reason he needed a difference engine?" Amelia's question hung in the dusty air like motes caught in a shaft of sunlight.

"Yes, as a matter of fact. He seemed quite energized about how he had discovered something about older technology. That he was onto something big, something that would change the way we view history," Pendergast recounted, a distant look crossing his craggy face. "He believed some ideas were too ahead of their time—waiting for the right moment, the right mind to resurrect them."

"Or the right maniac," Finn muttered under his breath.

"Excuse me?" Pendergast looked puzzled, the spectacles slipping further down his nose.

"Nothing, Mr. Pendergast," Finn said briskly. "What did you make of his ideas?"

"He didn't elaborate," Pendergast answered. "But if I had a penny for every person I've met who thinks that today's ills can be cured by forgotten technologies, I'd be a rich man. It never leads anywhere. Some people can't face up to the reality that there is no major cure hidden in the shadows for what ails us as human beings."

"Wait," Amelia interjected, her keen eyes catching a detail. She took out her phone and showed some photographs. "These notes were in a journal we found near Mr. Henshaw's body. Do they look like anything you'd know?"

"I'm no engineer," Pendergast chuckled, unaware of the gravity his words carried. "But that looks like some modification of an old counting machine. Possibly one of Babbage's own."

"Is there anything else you can tell us about Mr Henshaw?" Finn asked. "Where he was going, who he was dealing with?"

"I'm afraid not," Pendergast said with sadness. "But if Lucas Henshaw had a piece of a difference machine, you might want to see if anyone else has been collecting the pieces."

Finn nodded.

"One more thing," Amelia said. She showed another picture on her phone, this time of the pocket watch that was found in Lucas Henshaw's mouth. "Does this watch look familiar?"

"No," Mr. Pendergast said. "But I can date it for you. That looks to be from around the 1840s, given the style."

"The same period when Charles Babbage was making his prototype computers…" Amelia mused out loud.

"Yes," Pendergast said.

"And what about this?" Finn asked, pulling up a photo of the watch they found in the tree back at the cottage.

"Hmm," Pendergast said. "A little more difficult. I'd need to get my hands on it. The style could be Victorian, but there are some hints there that it's anachronistic, made much later but aping the Victorian style."

"But still the Victorian connection," Finn said, turning to Amelia. "I'm telling you, this is Vilne."

"Maybe," she answered. "But we've thought that before in other cases and it's turned out to be barely connected to him. I just want us to gather more evidence."

"Sometimes you have to go with your gut," Finn answered.

The door behind Finn and Amelia opened with a ring of the bell. A stout woman stepped in, smiling with rosy cheeks and then perusing the shop.

"If you don't mind," Pendergast said. "I think that's all I can say now. I have customers to tend to."

"Thank you, Mr. Pendergast. You've been most helpful," Finn said, nodding slightly.

"Anytime, Detective. Inspector. Do stop by if you wish to discuss Babbage further—or perhaps peruse our collection of horological wonders," Pendergast offered with a genial smile as they left.

Finn nodded with a grin. "This place is great."

"You don't have to ask him twice to come back," Amelia said. "Thank you again, Mr. Pendergast."

The phone in Finn's pocket buzzed insistently as they stepped out of Pendergast's dusty shop, the musty smell of old books and brass still clinging to them. He glanced at the screen, an anonymous number flashing up with a message that sent a chill down his spine.

"Amelia, it's another message. Look at it," Finn said, holding out the device for her to see. The text on the screen was a quote, antiquated in its language yet chillingly apt: "As cogs and gears do turn, the world prepares to burn."

"Another damned riddle," Amelia muttered, her face stoic with deep thoughts, clearly sifting through the implications.

Finn looked around.

"What is it?" Amelia asked.

"I get the feeling we're being watched," Finn answered. "The timing... We just came out of the place where Henshaw bought pieces of a difference machine, built with cogs and gears. Then, we get this. It's no coincidence."

"He could be anywhere," Amelia said. "Don't make it obvious you're looking. It's better if he thinks we're blind to it. Come on. Let's get back to the station."

***

Back at Hertfordshire Constabulary, Finn and Amelia sat in the dimly lit room, surrounded by stacks of case files and evidence bags. The air was heavy with the weight of unsolved mysteries and lingering danger. Finn's gaze was fixed on a series of photographs spread out before him, each one a piece of the puzzle they were trying to solve.

One image showed Lucas Henshaw's journal with intricate diagrams scrawled across its pages, hinting at a mind consumed by forgotten technologies. Another displayed the antique pocket watch found in Henshaw's mouth, its hands frozen in time. Finn's brow furrowed as he traced the connections between these relics of the past and the present-day murders.

Finn turned to another computer screen. On it was the moment of Emily Stanton's death, caught on camera for all the world to see. Alongside it was a text display of her viewers discussing the video in the chat window.

Finn and Amelia had both watched the video back now, over and over. Sadly, only the killer's mask could be seen for a brief second. It looked like a grotesque pale face caught in a frightening pose. But there was no way to identify the killer.

Amelia, on her part, sifted through notes detailing Pendergast's recollections of Henshaw and his acquisitions from the antiques dealer. She studied the receipt stained with blood, a grim reminder of lives intertwined by threads of history and technology.

Silence enveloped them as they absorbed the details before them, each lost in their own thoughts yet connected by an unspoken understanding. The flickering overhead light cast shadows that danced across their faces, mirroring the dance of shadows lurking in the depths of this intricate case.

Amelia's phone rang and she quickly picked up. "Winters... Yes... Okay, anything else? Thank you, Kelly. That's a big help." Amelia hung the phone up.

"What is it?" Finn asked.

"Preliminary tests show that both Emily and Lucas were murdered within 1 to 2 hours of each other."

Finn nodded.

"The killer must have prepared both kills well in advance to pull that off, rushing between scenes," Amelia said.

"I can't shake the feeling that there's a link between Lucas Henshaw and Emily Stanton," Finn mused, his eyes scanning the evidence before him. "Henshaw delved into archaic technology, seeking hidden truths in old machines, while Emily was all about modern tech, streaming her life for the world to see."

Amelia looked up from the notes she was reviewing, intrigued by Finn's train of thought. "You think their paths crossed somehow? That maybe Henshaw's pursuit of forgotten technologies led him to something that put him in the killer's sights?"

Finn nodded slowly, the pieces starting to align in his mind. "It's possible. Both of them were diving deep into realms where technology meets history. Henshaw with his antique devices and Emily with her online presence. Maybe there's a connection we're missing, something that ties them together beyond mere coincidence."

As they pondered this new angle, the weight of their investigation seemed to grow heavier, the shadows in the room deepening as if concealing secrets waiting to be uncovered. The clock on the wall ticked steadily, marking time as they delved deeper into the intertwined fates of Lucas Henshaw and Emily Stanton.

Amelia neatly stacked the notes she had been organizing, her fingers tracing over the details of their latest findings. As she closed the last folder, a sigh escaped her lips, mingling with the heavy air of the room that Finn felt was palpable.

Finn stretched in his chair, his muscles protesting from hours spent hunched over evidence. With an unexpected creak, the chair tipped backward, sending Finn sprawling to the floor with a thud. Startled, Amelia rushed to his side, extending a hand to help him up.

"Finn, are you alright?" concern laced her voice as she steadied him.

Finn grinned sheepishly as he got back on his feet, wanting to pass it off as deliberate. In a spontaneous move, he wrapped his arms around her waist and leaned in for a kiss. A blush crept up Amelia's cheeks as she gently pushed him back.

"Finn," she chided softly, "we can't... not here."

His smile remained warm as he nodded understandingly. "Of course, Amelia. I am, as always, a consummate professional."

Amelia took a moment to compose herself before suggesting their next course of action. "Before we call it a day, let's go speak with Emily Stanton's boyfriend. He might have more insights that could shed light on this tangled web we're unraveling."

Finn's gaze held hers for a lingering moment before he nodded in agreement. The unspoken understanding between them resonated in that shared look, a bond forged through countless cases and whispered confidences.

With resolve in their hearts and determination etched into their expressions, Finn and Amelia set off once more into the labyrinthine world of shadows and secrets that awaited them beyond the dimly lit room.

CHAPTER FIVE

Finn rapped sharply on the weathered door of Liam's apartment, the sound echoing down the dimly lit hallway. It swung open to reveal a figure that seemed to teeter on the edge of collapse, eyes red-rimmed and a week's worth of stubble lining his jaw.

"Mr. Holden?" Finn asked, though he already knew the answer.

"Y-yeah," Liam's voice was a hoarse whisper, "That's me."

"Detective Wright," Finn introduced himself, stepping inside with Amelia close behind. "This is Inspector Winters. We spoke with you earlier today. We're here about Emily."

"Oh, yes," he said, rubbing his temples as though he had only just awoken. "Come in."

The apartment reeked of stale beer and greasy food. Empty bottles clinked underfoot as they moved further into the chaos. Amelia's nose seemed wrinkled in distaste momentarily, but she remained silent, her gaze scanning the room with practiced detachment.

"Sorry 'bout the mess," Liam muttered, watching as Finn navigated through the detritus with careful steps. "Haven't really been up for cleaning today."

"Understandable," Finn said, his tone even, but not unkind. He stopped by a table littered with papers and picked up an old-fashioned pocket watch. "It's never easy to take in losing someone like this."

"I still don't believe it, I..." Liam couldn't finish the sentence, choking on his grief.

"We're sorry to disturb you," Amelia offered, gently. "But we need to go over a few things if we're to catch the person who killed Emily."

Liam nodded.

"Can you tell us about Emily's behavior lately?" Amelia asked in a professional tone. "Any changes that might suggest things were different for her?"

Liam wiped at his eyes with the back of his hand, then nodded slowly. "She was looking for a new angle for her live streams, Something to make her stand out. She got real deep into old books, essays." He gestured vaguely toward a shelf crammed with leather-bound volumes.

"Victorian novels?" Finn questioned, examining the spines of the books. Authors from another era gazed back at him through golden lettering.

"I think so," he answered. "But that wasn't really my kind of thing."

"And what would she do with this newfound interest?" Amelia asked.

"I think Emily thought she could do something where she visited Victorian locations and talk about them," Liam replied.

"With all respect," Finn added. "That doesn't sound like it would captivate a modern streaming audience. Did she have another angle?"

"Emily was interested in the macabre side of that time," Liam explained. "Her angle was strange stories of Victorian Britain. Murders, weird traditions, that sort of thing. People lap that up."

A thought crossed Finn's mind. "Weird traditions? Tell me, Liam, did Emily ever show interest in Victorian technology? Unusual inventions of the time, that sort of thing?"

"Yes, actually. And clocks, too. She started collecting them," Liam added, pointing towards a corner where a small array of antique timepieces sat. Their faces, frozen at different hours, seemed to mock the very concept of order.

"Clocks?" Amelia echoed, her curiosity piqued.

"Antique ones. Watches, too," Liam confirmed. "Got 'em all over the place."

"Did she ever say why this sudden interest?" Finn asked, studying Liam for any flicker of insight.

"Kept talking about lost time," Liam responded, his voice growing distant as if he were recalling a dream. "Like she wanted to touch the past or something. I'm more of a modern kind of guy, but it seemed to bring Emily joy, so how could it hurt? At least, that's what I thought."

"Mr. Holden," Amelia's voice cut through the heavy air of Liam's cluttered apartment, her gaze sharp and focused on him. "In the days leading up to Emily's murder, did she ever express any concerns about her safety? I know you mentioned that she sometimes received strange messages from viewers, but were there any unusual encounters or messages that specifically troubled her?"

Liam shifted uneasily, his eyes clouded with remembered worry. "There were some strange messages she got... from a guy named Tim Nolan."

Amelia's brows furrowed in recognition. "Tim Nolan? The one who writes those anti-technology pieces, criticizing our reliance on gadgets and gizmos?"

Liam nodded slowly, confirming her suspicion.

"I've heard of him," Amelia continued, her tone thoughtful. "Did Emily mention why Tim Nolan was reaching out to her? Any specific reasons for his messages?"

Liam ran a hand through his disheveled hair, his expression troubled. "She said he was targeting her online presence, accusing her of being part of the problem with society today. Kept going on about how technology was ruining everything."

Amelia's lips pressed into a thin line as she processed this information. "Did Emily engage with him? Respond to his accusations?"

Liam shook his head. "She tried to ignore most of it, but it weighed on her. Made her doubt what she was doing."

"Was Tim Nolan threatening in these messages?" Amelia probed further.

"Not directly," Liam clarified. "But there was this underlying menace in his words, like he knew something others didn't."

"Can we see the messages?" Finn asked.

"As far as I know," Liam answered, "Emily deletes her inbox. I wouldn't even know the password, anyway."

Amelia's gaze hardened at the implication. "Do you think Tim Nolan could have had anything to do with what happened to Emily?"

Liam hesitated before answering, uncertainty flickering across his features. "I don't know... I hope not. If it was him, I should have paid more attention to it."

As the weight of their conversation settled in the room like a shroud of suspicion, Amelia exchanged a significant glance with Finn before turning back to Liam, determination etched in every line of her face.

Finn stepped closer to the collection of timepieces, his fingers brushing over the cold brass of an ornate carriage clock. "You said she argued with Tim Nolan? Did Emily ever say anything public about him?"

"Right," Liam interjected, rubbing at his temple with a shaky hand. "Emily thought his fear of tech was a joke. Made a video about it and everything."

"Didn't go unnoticed, I take it?" Amelia's voice cut through the cluttered space as she sifted carefully through the detritus on a nearby coffee table.

"Hardly," Liam scoffed. "Nolan tore into her online. Called her names... said she was warping people's minds with her content." He shook his head, the shadow of a grimace playing on his lips.

"Did he ever pass on any poetry?" Finn pressed, eyes not leaving Liam's face.

"Poetry?" Liam sounded surprised. "Like a love letter or something?"

"No," Finn explained. "More like a cryptic message, perhaps about time and technology."

Liam nodded. "Emily did say he wrote like someone from the past. All flowery language. She said something about him calling her a 'slave to the machine and a soulless cog'." The bitterness in Liam's recitation hung heavy between them.

Finn nodded knowingly to Amelia, a flicker of recognition crossing his features as Liam's words echoed in his mind. The cryptic messages, the references to time and technology, it all sounded eerily familiar to the anonymous texts he had been receiving.

Amelia's gaze bore into Liam, her voice steady but piercing. "Do you think Tim Nolan could have known Emily was going to the Victorian Bathhouse where she was murdered?"

Liam shifted uncomfortably, his eyes darting around the room. "I... I don't know," he stammered.

Finn stepped in closer, his expression inscrutable. "Why do I get the feeling you know something about that? Did you tell Tim Nolan where she would be?"

Liam hesitated before finally nodding, a guilty look washing over his features. "I never messaged Nolan. But I did... I thought it would build hype for Emily's streams, get people talking about her, if I leaked some of the locations online ahead of time. I had no idea it might lead to this!"

"Why would you do that?" Amelia's question cut through the tension in the room.

"I wanted to help her succeed," Liam replied, his voice tinged with regret. "I never thought..."

Finn's skepticism was palpable as he interrupted, "You were trying to help by putting her in danger?"

Liam seemed genuinely distraught now, running a hand through his hair in frustration. "No! I didn't know... I didn't think anyone would..."

Amelia intervened gently, her tone reassuring yet firm. "No one is accusing you of anything."

Tears welled up in Liam's eyes as he struggled to compose himself. "Do you think they knew she was coming there? That they were waiting for her..."

Amelia's response was measured and calm. "We're still making inquiries into all possibilities, Liam."

Overwhelmed with guilt and sorrow, Liam broke down completely, his shoulders shaking with emotion.

Amelia placed a comforting hand on his shoulder. "We will catch whoever did this, Liam. You have our word."

As Amelia offered solace to the grieving man before them, Finn couldn't shake off the nagging feeling that there was more to Liam's actions than mere misguided attempts at promotion. His thoughts painted a darker picture than they had anticipated, but they hadn't coalesced into a theory.

Amelia looked at Finn, putting away her notebook.

"Thank you for your time, Mr. Holden," Amelia said with a respectful nod as they prepared to leave Liam's cluttered apartment.

"I'm sorry..." Liam sobbed.

"You'll get through this," Finn added. "But call us if you think of anything." He patted the man on the shoulder and left the room.

Stepping outside, the night had descended like a heavy curtain, casting shadows that danced in the glow of streetlights.

"We should call it a day," Amelia suggested, her breath misting in the chilly evening air. "We'll start fresh tomorrow by looking into Lucas Henshaw's life and questioning this Tim Nolan about his potential involvement."

Finn glanced at her thoughtfully before offering, "You could crash at my cottage tonight; it's closer than your new apartment."

Amelia hesitated for a moment before gently declining. "I appreciate it, Finn, but... I'd be worried what might happen if I did."

"Would that be so bad a thing?" Finn smiled, touching her cheek.

"I've never seen anyone else since my fiancé passed away. I need some time."

"You shouldn't feel guilt about that, Amelia," Finn offered. "I'm sure he would..."

34

"He would want me to move on," Amelia said with a sigh. "He was a good man... And so are you."

Understanding her unspoken request for space, Finn nodded quietly. "I don't want to push you into anything you're not ready for."

"I do want to be with you," Amelia said. "Just..."

"Not yet," Finn grinned. "I get it."

They stood under the dim glow of a nearby lamppost, their breath mingling with the crisp night air as they exchanged a silent understanding.

"Goodnight, Amelia," Finn said softly. "You know where I am if you change your mind."

"Goodnight, Finn," she replied before turning to head towards her car parked down the street.

CHAPTER SIX

The darkness of the night clung to Finn as he made his way towards his quaint cottage in Great Amwell, the gravel crunching beneath his boots like a whispered warning. A heavy silence hung in the air, disturbed only by the haunting hoot of an owl in the distance. As he drew closer to his front door, a patrol car sat ominously nearby, its red and blue lights painting the surrounding trees with an ethereal glow.

Inside the car, two police constables awaited, their faces half-shrouded in shadows but partially illuminated by the dashboard lights. Finn recognized them as officers from Chief Constable Collins' precinct.

"What's up, fellas?" Finn's voice cut through the eerie stillness, his breath forming ghostly wisps in the chilly night air.

The younger constable leaned towards the window to address Finn. "Orders from Chief Collins himself, sir. We're here to keep watch," he explained solemnly. "If Max Vilne shows up, he'll have to come through us first, Sir."

Finn acknowledged their duty with a nod. "It's usually quiet around here at night," he remarked before offering, "If you lads need anything—tea or a bite to eat—I've got some leftovers inside."

"Thank you, Sir," the younger constable said. "We'll keep that in mind. You have a good night."

Turning away from them, Finn pushed open his cottage door and stepped inside. A peculiar sense of emptiness washed over him despite soon having the crackling fire in the hearth; it felt as though shadows lingered where there should have been warmth and familiarity, unsettling whispers echoing off the walls like faint memories refusing to surface.

Finn poured himself a measure of whiskey, its amber glow casting a warm light in the dim room. The liquid swirled in the glass, a silent companion to his troubled thoughts. Max Vilne's recent visit to his haven flashed through Finn's mind, the chilling reminder of the effigies hanging ominously from that distant hill. Three figures dancing in the wind, taunting him with their twisted presence.

36

The weight of exhaustion settled heavily on Finn's shoulders as he contemplated whether he would ever find peace in sleep until Vilne was captured and locked away for good. Each creak of the cottage seemed to whisper Vilne's name, a spectral presence lingering in every corner.

Raising the glass to his lips, Finn took a slow sip, letting the fiery liquid burn momentarily before trailing warmth down his throat. The taste was sharp, grounding him in the reality of this relentless pursuit.

The crackling flames in the hearth danced with a mesmerizing rhythm, casting flickering shadows that played on Finn's tired face. As he sat in his favorite armchair, the amber glow of the fire painted the room in warm hues, creating a sanctuary from the cold night outside. His thoughts drifted to Amelia, his partner and confidante through the tumultuous events that had unfolded.

Amelia's grief weighed heavily on Finn's mind. He had been so consumed by his own quest for justice, chasing shadows and ghosts of the past, that he had neglected to truly see the pain she carried within her. The loss of her fiancé lingered like an unspoken specter between them, a wound that time alone could not heal.

Finn realized he had been selfish, too caught up in his own turmoil to offer Amelia the support she needed. She was strong and resilient, but even the strongest souls bore scars that ran deep. With a pang of regret, Finn understood that pushing her to open up about her feelings would only add to her burden.

Leaning back in his chair, Finn made a silent vow to himself. He would give Amelia space and time to navigate the labyrinth of emotions swirling within her. Their partnership was built on trust and understanding; he needed to respect her journey through grief without imposing his own solutions.

As he watched the flames crackle and dance, their warmth seeping into his bones, Finn knew that patience would be his greatest ally in supporting Amelia. In this quiet moment by the fire's gentle glow, he resolved to be there for her when she was ready to share her heartache.

Savoring another sip of whiskey, its fiery trail down his throat a bittersweet reminder of life's complexities, Finn let go of his impatience. The night stretched before him like an endless expanse of possibilities, each moment holding untold truths waiting to be unraveled.

Finn's thoughts shifted from the haunting shadows of his own struggles to the intricate web of the case at hand. The timing between Emily Stanton and Lucas Henshaw's deaths lingered in his mind like a cryptic puzzle waiting to be solved. How had the killer orchestrated such precise sequences of events, weaving a tapestry of death and mystery?

Lucas Henshaw's body, carefully bound to the spindle wheel in that abandoned mill, flashed vividly in Finn's memory. The macabre scene spoke volumes about the killer's meticulous nature, each knot and twist a deliberate act of cruelty. It was as if the murderer had choreographed a twisted ballet of demise, using Victorian elements as props in this grim performance.

The realization struck Finn with a chilling clarity. The killer must have calculated every move, every detail meticulously planned to ensure that Lucas Henshaw met his end before Emily Stanton fell victim at the bathhouse. The precision hinted at a mind steeped in darkness and methodical precision, orchestrating a symphony of death with sinister expertise.

The fiery liquid scorched a searing path down Finn's throat, the amber whiskey igniting a brief fire within him, momentarily distracting him from the relentless pursuit that consumed his thoughts. With a resolute clink, he placed the glass back on the table, its weighty thud echoing the burden of exhaustion that bore down on him like an invisible force.

Pushing himself up from his worn armchair, Finn muttered to himself under his breath, "Stay focused, Wright. You're getting closer." Each step he took towards his bedroom felt heavier than the last, the wooden staircase protesting with every creak as if whispering Vilne's name in the stillness of the night.

As he settled into bed, a palpable sense of solitude enveloped him, leaving a void beside him that seemed to ache with absence. He looked at it before closing his eyes—that emptiness next to him—and wondered about companionship. He remembered once being in love with his ex-fiance Demi, how he had been certain that they should marry. But time had eroded that certainty to the point where his feelings lay elsewhere, and deeply. Finn wondered what it would be like to go to sleep at night in the arms of Amelia, and to wake up with her face being the first to greet him.

He had once thought he knew love, but to his utter shock, his feelings for Amelia ran far deeper than that. Although he had hated hurting Demi by ending their relationship, he knew that it was the right thing to do, whether he ended up with Amelia or not.

This thought sent his mind down a nocturnal rabbit hole.

Drifting on the edge of consciousness, Finn's mind whirled with a flurry of thoughts and conjectures. What if there were not just one but two perpetrators orchestrating this intricate tapestry of murders? One to prey on Emily Stanton during her final moments broadcast live and another to meticulously design the elaborate crime scene where Lucas Henshaw met his demise.

"Could be..." Finn whispered to the night. "Easier to make the kills line up time-wise with two. One killer could have made the journey between both kills, but it would have been tight. Two makes more sense..."

This notion lingered in Finn's mind like a thick fog as sleep beckoned him into its embrace. In that hazy realm between wakefulness and dreams, Finn found himself conversing silently with himself.

"Are we dealing with two killers?" he mused aloud in his mind.

The idea unfurled before him like a delicate thread of investigation, challenging his preconceptions and unveiling a labyrinthine path fraught with unforeseen revelations waiting to be discovered. But those discoveries would have to wait for the dawn.

CHAPTER SEVEN

The elevator dinged open on the top floor of the Henshaw Technologies building, and Finn stepped out, his eyes instantly drawn to the vast expanse of glass and steel that framed the London skyline. Amelia followed close behind, her notebook gripped in her hand—a signal she was ready to dissect every word they would hear.

"A little more upmarket from the mill," Finn muttered, peering around at the minimalist decor of Lucas Henshaw's corporate headquarters. "Pendergast said Henshaw was successful, but I didn't think *this* successful."

"That wouldn't be hard," Amelia agreed, her tone dry as they approached the reception desk. "But there's money here, and where there's money, there's motive."

"Detective Wright and Inspector Winters to see Mr. Henshaw's representative," Finn announced to the young woman tapping away at a keyboard behind the desk. She glanced up, her eyes flicking between them before nodding towards the corridor to their left.

"Second door. His executive assistant, Ms. Corbin, will meet you there."

"Thank you," Amelia said with a polite smile, leading the way.

The door to Henshaw's office clicked open before they could knock, revealing a woman in her thirties, impeccably dressed, her face set in a professional mask.

"Ms. Corbin?" Finn asked, extending a hand.

"Indeed. You're here about Mr. Henshaw's... unfortunate demise?"

"Right in one," Finn replied, catching the brief flicker of distress crossing her features. Amelia dove straight in.

"Ms. Corbin, do you happen to know if Mr. Henshaw had any enemies or anyone who might have wanted to harm him?" Amelia inquired, her gaze steady.

Ms. Corbin paused for a moment, considering the question carefully. "No one specific comes to mind, Detective. Mr. Henshaw was a prominent figure in the business community, and one doesn't rise to his level without stepping on a few toes along the way," she replied with a hint of somber reflection.

Finn interjected, "Was Mr. Henshaw known for being particularly competitive with other businesses?"

Ms. Corbin hesitated briefly before responding, "It's possible that he may have pushed boundaries at times. Success in this world often demands such actions."

Amelia pressed further, her curiosity piqued. "What do you mean by 'pushing boundaries'? Could you elaborate on that?"

A guarded expression crossed Ms. Corbin's face as she maintained her professional demeanor. "I'm afraid I can't divulge much more on internal company matters beyond stating that competition in our industry can be fierce."

Finn observed Ms. Corbin's reaction keenly, noting the subtle shift in her demeanor as he decided to delve into a more specific line of questioning.

"Ms. Corbin, are you aware of a particular item Mr. Henshaw purchased recently? A... 'difference engine,' if that rings any bells?" Finn inquired, watching for any flicker of recognition in her eyes.

Ms. Corbin's composure wavered slightly at the mention of the difference engine, a hint of defensiveness creeping into her tone. "Detective, I'm afraid I can't discuss Mr. Henshaw's private projects or acquisitions," she replied, her voice firm but betraying a trace of unease.

A small grin played on Finn's lips as he leaned back slightly in his chair. "Ah, so there is indeed a project revolving around the difference engine?" Finn prodded gently, observing how Ms. Corbin's facade faltered for a split second.

Ms. Corbin stumbled over her words momentarily, regaining her professional poise as she denied any knowledge of such a project. "I... I quite... I quite assure you, Detective Wright, Mr. Henshaw's focus was primarily on the company's technological advancements and business strategies," she stated firmly, though a subtle tension lingered in the air between them.

Amelia's gaze sharpened, a glint of steel in her eyes as she leaned in slightly towards Ms. Corbin. "Ms. Corbin, we appreciate your cooperation thus far. However, if we suspect any obstruction in our investigation, we won't hesitate to bring you in for questioning," she stated firmly but with a calculated edge.

Ms. Corbin's composed facade cracked ever so slightly at the implied threat. Lowering her voice, she met Amelia's unwavering stare and asked, "What do you want to know?" Her tone held a mix of wariness and guarded curiosity, hinting at hidden layers beneath her professional demeanor.

Finn observed the subtle power play between the two women, his detective instincts on high alert as he noted the shift in dynamics. It was a delicate dance of words and intentions, each move calculated to reveal just enough without giving away too much.

Amelia's next question hung in the air like a silent challenge, her voice cool and measured. "Tell us about Mr. Henshaw's interest in Victorian technology."

Ms. Corbin hesitated, her gaze darting to the now-closed office door. "I'm not privy to all the details. Lucas—Mr. Henshaw—was very secretive about it. Said it was going to change the tech world. Most of us were skeptical."

"Seems like a lot of secrets for an open-plan office," Finn quipped, but his eyes were serious. He noticed the tension in Ms. Corbin's posture, the way her fingers played with the pen in her hand.

Ms. Corbin stood up and walked towards another door. "Whatever he was working on, Lucas spent hours in here," she said, finally opening the door to let them into the inner sanctum of Lucas Henshaw. "Alone, mostly. I don't think anyone truly knew what he was onto."

The office was a shrine to contemporary design, sleek lines, and muted colors; a large desk dominated the space, surrounded by various digital screens. Yet, there was an absence, a sense of something hidden beneath the surface.

"Old books and diagrams, is that right?" Amelia pressed, her keen eyes scanning the room as if she could conjure the secrets from the walls themselves.

"Yes, quite the departure from his usual work," Ms. Corbin confessed. "He had a safe where he kept things... away from prying eyes."

Finn walked over to the expansive window, hands in his pockets, turning back to face Ms. Corbin. "Mind if we take a look at this safe?"

"Without a warrant?" she challenged, though her voice wavered slightly.

"It's better this way," Finn said, firmly. "Otherwise, we come in here and go over everything this company is sitting on, and that could get very messy, especially if you don't want Mr Henshaw's fascination with older tech getting into the public eye."

"You're perceptive," Ms. Corbin grinned. "If I'm honest, I thought Lucas was going mad. Why would a tech innovator look to the past with such glee? Clocks. Old cogs and gears. It's so outdated."

"And we're people in the boardroom worried about this newfound interest?" Amelia asked.

"It was a concern for everyone," Ms. Corbin said. "Lucas was the face of the company. His charisma and self-belief were what fueled the company's meteoric rise."

"Let's not sully you're company then," Finn said, pointing to the back of the office, where a suspicious, overly-sized painting hung on a wall.

"Consider it a courtesy to avoid further disruption," Amelia interjected smoothly. "We'll be in and out."

With a sigh, Ms. Corbin relented, moving to a painting hanging askew and revealing a state-of-the-art wall safe. She punched in a code, and the door swung open.

"Wouldn't have pegged him for a fan of Victoriana," Finn observed, cocking his head as he peered inside the safe without touching anything. Books with worn spines, rolled-up diagrams, and a scattering of notes were visible.

"Lucas was obsessed, but brilliant," Ms. Corbin said, a touch of fondness creeping into her voice before it hardened again.

"Would you be averse to us going through some of these?" Finn asked.

"As far as I'm concerned," Ms. Corbin began, "the further Lucas's flights of fancy are away from the company, the better the chances are that there will still be a company for me to work at. Knock yourself out."

Finn pulled on some forensics gloves and then carefully pulled out the documents and parchments. Amelia then revealed an evidence bag, which she unfolded and held open as Finn placed the items inside of it.

Finn's mind now went to the second thread they needed to pull in the case—the anti-futurist, Tim Nolan. The man who had sent threatening messages to Emily Stanton. Finn felt that there must be a connection.

"Did Lucas ever mention someone named Tim Nolan?" Finn asked, watching her reaction closely.

"Can't say he did," she responded, her brow furrowing. "Should he have?"

"He's an anti-tech blogger," Amelia explained. "We believe that he may be connected to some of this."

"The murderer?" Ms. Corbin asked.

"We wouldn't go that far," answered Amelia. "But a person of interest, and we wondered if Lucas had any dealings with him."

"I've never heard that name, sorry. Will there be anything else?"

"Would you be averse to us looking around here?" Finn asked.

"I don't think…" Ms. Corbin started. But Finn sensed that the protest wouldn't hold.

"As I said before, we'll just get a warrant, Ms. Corbin," Finn explained. "And that's a hassle, especially if the press get wind of us coming into your offices through legal force. It would be much better for the company, and for you, if we are able to quietly go about our business."

Ms. Corbin glared at Finn for a moment. "Okay, but don't tell the other board members, and please be quick."

"Thank you, Ms. Corbin," Amelia said.

Ms. Corbin turned and left the room.

Finn looked around. The room beyond was a dim cave of modernity—glass and chrome reflecting the sun outside. Amelia slipped in behind him, her presence a silent shadow that mirrored his own caution.

"Lucas clearly had a thing for the past," Finn murmured, sweeping his gaze over several shelves lined with leather-bound books, titles embossed in gold declaring their Victorian heritage.

Finn's gaze swept over the shelves, lined with leather-bound books that seemed to whisper of a bygone era. Among them, an old, worn book caught his eye. Its spine bore the name "Ezra Bellamy" in faded gold letters, triggering a surge of recognition deep within Finn's memory.

Turning to Amelia, Finn's eyes lit up with realization. "I know this name," he said quietly but with a sense of urgency coloring his tone. "Ezra Bellamy... I remember seeing it among the books at Emily Stanton's house."

Amelia's face broke into a rare grin, her eyes alight with the thrill of progress in their investigation. "Finally, we have a connection," she exclaimed softly. "But who is Ezra Bellamy?"

"Let me see what we took from the safe, please," Finn asked.

Amelia removed the books and parchments from the evidence bag in her hand, laying them out on the desk. Finn's gaze lingered on one particular book with a weathered cover. He picked it up, flipping through the pages before his eyes widened in recognition.

"This one, too," Finn pointed out, showing Amelia the name inscribed on the title page. "It's by Ezra Bellamy as well."

Amelia studied the book closely, her brow furrowed in concentration. "We'll need to find out who Ezra Bellamy is," she stated firmly, her mind already racing with possibilities as they delved deeper into the mysterious connections surrounding Lucas Henshaw's hidden pursuits.

"Look at this parchment," she said, picking up on the drawings of intricate gears and springs. "This looks similar to the drawings we found at the old mill. He must have been deep into whatever he was working on. "

"Too deep," Finn agreed, thumbed through the book by Ezra Bellamy. The book was ancient, its pages yellowed and delicate, but what drew Finn's attention were the feverish notes scribbled in the margins.

"Amelia, check this out." He pointed at a passage in the journal. "Our friend Lucas was not just a casual reader."

"Seems he fancied himself a decoder of sorts," Amelia said, leaning in closer to inspect the annotations. Numbers, symbols, and equations formed a chaotic constellation around the text.

"But without a codex, I doubt we can decipher what it means," Amelia mused.

"Here," Finn tapped on a note that stood out amongst the mathematical maelstrom. "'The Tempus Machine - key to control?' What do you make of that?"

"Tempus... I think that means Time in Latin," Amelia offered, her voice low. "A tempus machine would then infer something that controls time itself. Ms. Corbin was right, Lucas Henshaw really had lost his mind. A time machine? It's like something out of a steampunk novel."

"Look at this," Finn murmured, revealing hand transcribed notes on a piece of paper tucked inside one of the books. "Our man Lucas wasn't the only one with flights of fancy. This is the same handwriting, and it looks like Lucas was working alongside someone else."

Finn pointed to a passage that read 'Chronos knows. Must ask him about differential gear slip. Won't work without it. But don't trust him. Need to be careful.'

Amelia leaned in closer, her breath making its presence known on the back of Finn's neck. "Who is it?" she asked.

45

"Someone who goes by 'Chronos,'" he replied, scrolling through the exchanges.

"Isn't that another reference to the past?" Amelia asked. "I think Chronos was a Titan in Greek mythology."

"Different spelling," Finn said. He pulled out his phone and quickly searched for the name. He then read out loud what he had found. "I thought I'd heard of it. Chronos was a deity of sorts, he was the keeper of time itself. The being that kept time moving."

"A bit of a dramatic name," Amelia said. "Much like our killer's flair for the dramatic."

"Agreed," Finn said. "But look, on the same page. There are coordinates."

"We should put them into our maps app," Amelia suggested.

"Already on it." Finn's eyes didn't leave the screen as his fingers danced across the screen. The room around them faded into background noise—the hum of electronics, the soft wheeze of the air conditioning system—all underscored by the relentless ticking of the clock on the wall.

"Got a location," Finn announced, a satisfied smirk tugging at his lips.

"Where does it lead us?" Amelia's voice held a mix of anticipation and dread.

"Let's find out." Finn pulled up a map on the screen, plotting the coordinates. A red dot blinked into existence, marking their destination. "A house on the outskirts of Bingham Town. Looks like it's Victorian."

"Of course, it is," Amelia said, pushing away from the desk with a sigh. "Let's go pay a visit to our mysterious 'Chronos.'"

CHAPTER EIGHT

The drive to the location was silent, save for the occasional crackle of the police radio. When they arrived at the derelict Victorian house, the sight before them seemed to echo the madness of the case. The once grand structure loomed like a specter against the gray sky, its windows darkened with age and neglect.

"Charming place," Finn remarked dryly as they stepped out of the car.

"Time hasn't been kind to it," Amelia observed, approaching the entrance with caution.

"Neither have the owners, apparently." Finn followed suit, his hand instinctively wishing for the gun that wasn't there.

The front door creaked open at their touch, revealing a foyer draped in cobwebs and dust. But it wasn't the decay that sent shivers down Finn's spine—it was the sound. The house was alive with ticking, a cacophony of clocks chiming in eerie unison.

"Look at this," Amelia whispered, her flashlight beam sweeping across the walls lined with timepieces. Grandfather clocks stood sentinel beside delicate mantel clocks, each one meticulously set to the same time.

"Seems our 'Chronos' has a thing for punctuality," Finn said, stepping further into the house, his senses alert.

"Watch your step, Finn," Amelia replied, her tone laced with caution.

Together, they delved deeper into the labyrinthine corridors of the house. Finn couldn't shake off the unease crawling under his skin, nor the feeling that, with each tick of the clocks, they were being inexorably drawn into the intricate workings of a plan far beyond their comprehension.

The descent into the basement was like stepping backward in time. The musty air grew thick with the scent of oil and metal as Finn led the way, flashlight cutting through the darkness. Amelia's steps on the wooden stairs echoed behind him, steady and cautious.

"Feels like we're walking straight into a Jules Verne novel," she murmured.

"Or a trap," Finn said, his voice low. He paused at the bottom step, scanning the expanse before them. The beam of his flashlight swept across a haphazard sprawl of machinery and tools that looked as if they had been plucked straight from the industrial revolution.

"Look at this," Amelia said, her light landing on a wall adorned with blueprints. She stepped closer, tracing a finger along the lines of the intricate design. "The Tempus Machine! Just like in Lucas Henshaw's notes."

Finn joined her, eyes narrowing as he studied the plans. "Maybe that's what this is all about, people trying to get their hands on that old technology."

Next to the blueprints were swirling drawings of clocks moving backwards.

"Trying to turn back time?" Amelia questioned, skepticism tinged with a hint of dread in her tone. "This is madness."

"Or something even more ambitious," Finn replied, his analytical mind piecing together the implications of such a device.

Their contemplation was shattered by a sudden clatter. Spinning around, Finn caught sight of a shadow darting between the machinery.

"Show yourself!" Amelia called out, her own weapon drawn.

Silence, then the grinding sound of gears, and a figure emerged from the shadows. It was a man, or at least, it seemed to be. Clad in dark, tattered clothing reminiscent of a Victorian factory worker, he wore a gas mask with glass eyes that reflected their flashlight beams like a nocturnal creature caught in headlights. In his hand gleamed a large brass-handled knife.

"Ah, detectives," the figure rasped through the filter of his mask, the words distorted but chillingly articulate. "Welcome to the heart of the great work."

"Put down the knife," Finn commanded, pointing steadily at the masked assailant. "We can talk about this."

"Talk?" The figure chuckled, a hollow sound that reverberated off the stone walls. "There is no need for words when time itself will soon be rewritten!"

In a flash of movement, the attacker lunged, knife arcing through the air towards them. Amelia dodged to one side, while Finn parried the strike with his arm, feeling the jolt run up to his shoulder.

"Amelia, a little help!" Finn barked, grappling with the attacker. The man was strong, fueled by manic fervor.

"Trying!" Amelia shouted back, circling behind the assailant. She aimed a kick at his knee, sending him stumbling forward.

"Enough of this!" Finn growled, using the man's momentary imbalance to wrench the knife from his grip and send it skittering across the floor.

"Your efforts are futile," the masked figure spat, even as he tried to regain his footing. "The machine will be completed, and the world set right!"

"Pal, I've heard some delusions in my time, but this one takes the gold medal," Finn pressed, pushing the man against the wall.

The masked figure's blank eyes gleamed with fervor as he reached for his belt, pulling out a curved dagger that glinted malevolently in the dim light. With a swift, calculated motion, he lunged towards Finn, the blade finding its mark on Finn's exposed forearm. A sharp pain shot through Finn as he grunted in response to the unexpected attack.

Blood welled up around the wound, staining his sleeve crimson as the room filled with the metallic tang of fresh blood. The assailant's twisted smile widened beneath the eerie gas mask as Finn staggered back, his hand instinctively clutching at the searing injury. The ticking of the clocks seemed to blend with Finn's racing heartbeat, creating a dissonant symphony of danger and urgency in the air.

Amelia lunged forward, aiming to grab the masked man, but before she could reach him, his fist swung out with surprising speed, catching her square on the jaw. Finn watched in horror as the impact clearly sent a shockwave of pain through her head, and she stumbled back, gritting her teeth against the throbbing ache.

As the assailant darted away, Amelia shook off the dizziness and steadied herself. "Finn, are you okay?" she called out, concern lacing her voice as she saw him clutching his bleeding arm.

"I'll manage. Stay here," Finn replied through clenched teeth, his eyes fixed on the fleeing figure disappearing up a rickety staircase that groaned under each step he took.

"Like hell," Amelia answered, holding her bloodied nose.

"Please," Finn said, softly.

Amelia watched Finn's determined form disappear up the dilapidated stairs. The wood creaked and protested under their weight as he ascended with agile urgency, his senses sharp and focused on capturing their elusive prey.

The dim light filtering through cracked windows cast long shadows that danced along the walls as Finn pursued the masked man higher into the decaying structure. The air grew heavier with dust and neglect, but Finn pressed on, adrenaline lending strength to his steps.

At the top of the staircase, Finn caught sight of a tattered curtain billowing in an unseen draft. Without hesitation, he pushed past it into a room filled with broken furniture and faded wallpaper peeling off like old skin.

The masked man stood at the far end of the room, his breath ragged beneath the mask as he turned to face Finn with manic determination in his stance. Before any words could be exchanged between them, he made a desperate leap through a shattered window overlooking the overgrown backyard below.

"Finn!" Amelia's voice echoed from below as she reached the top of the staircase behind him.

Ignoring her call for caution, Finn rushed to the window just in time to see their quarry disappearing into the misty landscape beyond. Without hesitation, he made a split-second decision and followed suit, leaping out into open air without looking back.

The ground rushed up to meet him as branches clawed at his clothes and brambles tore at his skin. Pain shot through him upon landing but was quickly forgotten as he scrambled to his feet and resumed pursuit through tangled bushes and twisted trees that seemed to reach out like skeletal fingers in pursuit of their own.

Thorns and brambles tore at Finn's clothes and skin as he pushed through the dense undergrowth, his heart pounding in sync with the frantic rustling of leaves around him. The masked man's ragged breaths echoed ahead, a taunting reminder of his ever-elusive presence.

Each step forward felt like a battle against nature itself, the twisted branches clawing at him as if trying to hold him back. Finn gritted his teeth against the stinging pain of scratches left in their wake, a visceral trail marking his relentless pursuit.

The air was thick with the earthy scent of damp soil and decay, a suffocating embrace that seemed to close in on him with each passing second. Shadows danced wildly among the gnarled trees, casting fleeting glimpses of movement that played tricks on Finn's senses.

Branches cracked underfoot like gunshots, a cacophony of sound that masked any hint of the masked man's whereabouts. Panic threatened to bubble up within Finn's chest, but he ruthlessly suppressed it, focusing solely on closing the distance between them.

A sudden clearing emerged ahead, bathed in the gray light from above that illuminated the figure darting across it. Finn's muscles tensed as he quickened his pace, determination lending speed to his pursuit despite the burning ache in his limbs.

The masked man vanished into a tangle of thicket beyond the clearing, leaving only a fleeting shadow behind. Finn surged forward, adrenaline fueling his every move as he plunged into the darkness after his quarry.

The ground beneath his feet shifted from soft moss to unforgiving gravel, sending sharp jolts of pain up his legs with each hurried step. The distant sound of rushing water filled the night air, adding an ominous backdrop to their deadly game of cat and mouse.

Finn's breath came in ragged gasps now, sweat mingling with blood on his brow as he forced himself onward. The masked man was close; he could feel it like a primal instinct urging him towards an inevitable confrontation.

As he burst through another thicket into a wet glade ahead, Finn caught sight of the figure disappearing into what looked to be an old, overgrown hedged maze. The thick, verdant walls of the overgrown maze loomed around Finn as he plunged into its labyrinthine depths. The scent of crushed foliage mingled with the metallic tang of blood seeping from his arm, a stark reminder of the perilous chase he was embroiled in. Each twist and turn seemed to mock him, leading him further into the heart of the tangled greenery where shadows danced like specters in the fading light.

His boots crunched on fallen leaves and snapped twigs, a cacophony that drowned out even the sound of his own ragged breaths. The laughter, eerie and taunting, echoed through the hedges, spurring Finn on despite the growing ache in his limbs. He gritted his teeth against both physical pain and mounting frustration, determination etched into every line of his face.

The masked man's mocking chuckles seemed to play tricks on Finn's senses, bouncing off the leafy walls and leading him deeper into the maze's embrace. With each step forward, it felt as though he was descending further into a nightmarish world where reality blurred with illusion. But Finn refused to yield to doubt; he pushed forward with unwavering resolve.

Sunlight filtered weakly through gaps in the dense foliage above, casting dappled patterns on the moss-covered ground beneath Finn's feet. The air grew cooler as he ventured deeper into the heart of the maze, tendrils of mist curling around him like ghostly fingers. His pulse quickened with a mix of adrenaline and urgency as he strained to catch any glimpse of movement ahead.

A sharp turn brought Finn face-to-face with a dead end—a wall of thick bushes that seemed impenetrable. But just as panic threatened to claw its way up from within him, a faint rustling sound caught his attention. Without hesitation, he pressed onward, parting branches with a fierce determination that bordered on desperation.

The laughter grew louder now, reverberating through the confined space like a lingering echo from some malevolent source. It spurred Finn on like a beacon in the gloom of the overcast day, guiding him towards an inevitable confrontation with his elusive quarry. Blood dripped steadily from his wound, marking his trail through the verdant maze like a macabre breadcrumb path.

As Finn rounded another corner, he caught a fleeting glimpse of movement ahead—a flash of dark fabric disappearing behind a thicket obscured by creeping vines. His heart hammered in his chest as he surged forward once more, heedless of scratches and bruises acquired along this harrowing pursuit.

With each passing moment, Finn felt as though time itself had slowed to a crawl within this twisted green labyrinth. The masked man's laughter now rang out clear and chillingly close—a siren call laced with malice that drove Finn onwards despite every instinct screaming for caution.

And so Finn pressed deeper into the maze's winding corridors, determined to confront this shadowy figure whose twisted game had led them both down this treacherous path towards an inevitable reckoning.

The maze's twisting paths finally led Finn to its heart, a small clearing where an ancient sundial stood sentinel amidst the encroaching greenery. The weathered stone bore the ominous inscription, 'All shall be undone,' etched into its surface with an air of foreboding permanence. Finn's gaze lingered on the words, a chill creeping up his spine despite the warmth of the fading sunlight.

Silence enveloped him like a suffocating shroud as he scanned his surroundings, straining to catch any hint of movement or sound. The only response was the gentle rustle of leaves in the breeze and the distant call of a solitary bird. No mocking laughter, no taunting presence—just an empty stillness that whispered of escape.

In that moment, a heavy certainty settled in Finn's soul like a lead weight. The masked man had slipped through his grasp, leaving behind only cryptic words and unanswered questions. A surge of frustration mingled with resignation as he realized the futility of this pursuit.

With a heavy sigh, Finn closed his eyes briefly, centering himself amidst the fading light and encroaching shadows. The realization sank in—he had been outmaneuvered by a phantom in the maze's twisting corridors, left to decipher cryptic messages while his quarry slipped away into obscurity.

"Finn!" a welcome voice cried out somewhere nearby.

"Amelia!" Finn's voice echoed through the dense foliage, carrying a mix of relief and urgency. He strained to hear her response over the rustling leaves and his own ragged breaths.

"I'm in the maze!" Finn shouted back, his words swallowed by the verdant walls that seemed to close in around him. The distant sound of Amelia's voice calling out spurred him on, a lifeline in the labyrinthine darkness.

"Follow my voice, Finn!" Her command cut through the oppressive silence like a beacon, guiding him towards salvation. With renewed determination, he pressed forward, each step bringing him closer to her reassuring presence.

As he followed the sound of her voice, Finn's heart raced with a mix of anticipation and dread. The twisting paths seemed to conspire against him, leading him deeper into the maze's enigmatic embrace. But Amelia's unwavering guidance kept him focused on escape.

Finally, after what felt like an eternity of winding corridors and dead ends, Finn burst into a small clearing where sunlight filtered weakly through the canopy above. There stood Amelia, her gaze fixed on him with unspoken relief as he emerged from the shadows, her face bloodied from the encounter with the masked man.

Amelia's eyes locked with Finn's, revealing a mix of relief and exhaustion in their depths. Without a word, he closed the distance between them, wrapping her in a tight embrace. The rush of adrenaline from their pursuit still pulsed through him.

"Are you alright?" Finn's voice was gruff with worry.

"I don't think my nose is broken, but an ice pack wouldn't hurt," Amelia replied calmly, her resilience a constant source of awe for Finn. "You can grab me one."

Releasing her from the hug, Finn motioned towards their police car, his arm instinctively draping over her shoulders for support, both physical and emotional. The weight of what they had just witnessed lingered heavily between them.

"It's terrible to imagine that the gas-masked figure was the last sight Emily Stanton and Lucas Henshaw beheld," Amelia spoke softly, sorrow coloring her tone as she mourned the victims' untimely ends.

As they approached the vehicle, a nagging thought gnawed at Finn's mind. "I think there might be more than one perpetrator out there," he confessed to Amelia, an unsettling feeling washing over him like a shroud.

"Two?" Amelia asked, her voice fraught with unease.

"Maybe," Finn said. "I have a feeling that this Tempus machine stuff, as crazy as it is, is some sort of cult. Who knows what they might be working on?"

"You don't actually believe in this stuff, do you?" Amelia said.

"It doesn't matter if I believe," Finn answered, his voice stoic. "All that matters is that *they* do. That's enough to make them more dangerous than anything we've ever faced together."

CHAPTER NINE

The train carriage lay cloaked in shadows, the flickering paraffin lamps casting dancing silhouettes on the rusted metal walls. The air inside was thick with neglect, carrying hints of decay that lingered heavily around the killer as he moved through the narrow corridor. Each step he took echoed softly, blending with the eerie symphony of creaks and groans that seemed to echo ancient secrets within the carriage.

His hand brushed against cold, metallic doors as he passed by sealed compartments, their windows boarded up tightly, trapping forgotten histories within. Finally reaching the end of the carriage, a sense of anticipation coiled in his chest as he pushed open a door that protested with a faint squeal from rusty hinges.

Inside, dust motes danced in dim light filtering through grimy windows, revealing a scene frozen in time. An old leather-bound book rested on a weathered seat, its yellowed pages bearing the name Ezra Bellamy. The significance of the name sent a thrill down his spine.

Opening the book revealed intricate script detailing arcane knowledge and forbidden secrets. Each page pulsed with hidden power, drawing him further into its mysterious allure. Symbols danced before his eyes, weaving tales of ancient wisdom and dark intent.

As he delved deeper into its pages, a sense of connection thrummed through him like an electric current. This was more than just a book; it held promises of control and dominance over those who dared defy its words.

A malevolent grin twisted his lips as he absorbed the knowledge within those pages, feeling an exhilarating rush course through his veins. The world would soon bow before him under forces beyond mortal understanding.

In this forgotten corner of London's underground labyrinth, amidst shadows and whispers of bygone eras, the killer embraced his destiny with newfound clarity. Armed with Ezra Bellamy's legacy, he prepared to wield unimaginable power to fulfill their shared vision.

Closing the book reverently, he tucked it securely under his arm as he readied to leave this eerie sanctuary behind. The echoes of past deeds lingered in the air around him as he stepped out into darkness once more, emboldened by what lay ahead on this fateful night.

In the dim light of the abandoned train carriage, the killer reached into the inner pocket of his coat and retrieved a crumpled sheet of paper. Unfolding it with deliberate care, his eyes scanned the list of names scrawled in elegant script. Each name held significance, each individual marked for a purpose only he understood.

A chilling smile crept across his face as he whispered to himself, the words barely more than a breath in the stagnant air. "All with the special knowledge must die, so that the Tempus Machine can live."

The weight of his mission bore down on him like a mantle of darkness, fueling his resolve with an unholy fervor. The power promised by the Tempus Machine was too great to allow any who possessed such forbidden knowledge to stand in its way.

With each name on that list, he saw not individuals but obstacles to be eradicated for the greater cause he served. The fate of those marked by his hand was sealed in ink and blood, their existence now tied irrevocably to the machinations of time and destiny.

As he refolded the paper and tucked it back into his pocket, a sense of purpose coursed through him like a malevolent current. The shadows whispered their approval as he prepared to execute his grim task, ensuring that no one would hinder the rise of a new era under the dominion of the Tempus Machine.

Moving with a purposeful stride, the killer left behind the dusty confines of the eerie train carriage and ventured deeper into the labyrinth of forgotten history. The dim light flickered as he approached another compartment, its door slightly ajar as if beckoning him inside.

Pushing it open, he was met with a chilling display that sent a thrill down his spine. Adorning the walls were an array of weapons from antiquity, each bearing the weight of past violence and untold stories. Among them, a small scythe-like blade caught his attention, its edge gleaming in the muted light like a promise of retribution.

Without hesitation, he reached out and grasped the blade, feeling its cold steel bite into his skin. A bead of crimson welled up from his finger, marking a silent covenant between weapon and wielder. The sharp point drew blood, igniting a visceral thrill that pulsed through him like a dark heartbeat.

As he stared at the blade stained with his own essence, an image flashed before his eyes - the weapon plunging into the soft flesh of his next victim with deadly precision. The anticipation of that moment sent shivers of delight down his spine, fueling his twisted desires with every beat of his heart.

Driven by macabre fascination, he donned an old Victorian mask hanging nearby, its cracked surface whispering tales of long-forgotten masquerades and hidden identities. The mask transformed him into a phantom of the past, obscuring his features behind an unsettling facade that promised both anonymity and dread.

With newfound purpose coursing through his veins and the taste of blood lingering on his lips, he stepped out of the compartment like a specter emerging from shadows. The killer moved with silent intent, blending seamlessly into the darkness as if becoming one with it.

In that fleeting moment before vanishing completely from sight, he embraced his role as an agent of chaos and death in this intricate dance orchestrated by forces beyond mortal comprehension. With every step taken in that ancient carriage echoing tales untold, he embarked on a journey to fulfill destiny's grim design under the watchful gaze of time itself.

CHAPTER TEN

Finn winced as the needle pierced his skin, the sharp sting of the anesthesia a harsh reminder of his recent scuffle. The sterile smell of antiseptic filled the small room at the Hertfordshire Constabulary where they were being patched up. He watched as Amelia sat across from him, an ice pack pressed against her nose, a faint bruise already blossoming on her cheek.

"Guess we're quite the pair today," Finn remarked, trying to lighten the mood despite the throbbing ache in his arm.

Amelia shot him a wry smile, her eyes glinting with a mix of amusement and exasperation. "You always manage to get yourself into trouble, don't you?"

"It's all part of my charm," Finn quipped, earning a chuckle from Amelia that turned into a wince as she shifted uncomfortably.

The paramedic attending to them raised an eyebrow at their banter but wisely chose not to comment as he focused on stitching up Finn's wound with practiced precision.

"How's the nose holding up?" Finn asked, tilting his head slightly to get a better look at her injury.

Amelia shrugged lightly. "Could be worse. At least it's not broken this time."

Finn nodded in agreement, grateful that their injuries weren't more severe given the dangerous nature of their work. As the paramedic finished up with Finn's stitches, he turned his attention back to Amelia.

"You know," Finn began, a mischievous glint in his eyes, "I think this might just be our most glamorous crime scene yet."

Amelia rolled her eyes but couldn't hide a smirk. "Oh yes, nothing says glamour like getting attacked by Victorian-obsessed murderers in dilapidated old buildings."

"Exactly," Finn replied with mock seriousness. "We're living every detective's dream."

The paramedic cleared his throat discreetly, signaling that they were both good to go. Finn flexed his newly stitched arm experimentally while Amelia removed the ice pack from her nose and tested its soreness with a gentle touch.

"Well," Amelia said as she stood up, readjusting her jacket, "back to the grindstone then?"

Finn followed suit and got to his feet with a nod. "Thank you."

The bustling London street greeted Finn and Amelia with a cacophony of sounds and a whirlwind of activity. Pedestrians hurried past, their footsteps echoing on the cobblestones, while the distant honking of cars added to the urban symphony. Neon lights from storefronts cast a vibrant glow, illuminating the eclectic mix of shops that lined the narrow road.

Finn adjusted his coat, feeling the weight of recent events still lingering in the air around them. Amelia walked beside him, her gaze sharp and focused as they navigated through the throng of people. Despite the chaos of the city, a sense of camaraderie settled between them, forged through shared danger and unwavering determination.

As they made their way through the crowded sidewalk, Finn caught sight of a street performer playing a haunting melody on a violin. The mournful notes seemed to echo the somber mood that clung to them like a shadow. Amelia glanced at Finn briefly before returning her attention to their surroundings, her eyes scanning for any signs that could lead them closer to unraveling the mysteries that had entwined their lives.

A sudden gust of wind swept down the street, carrying with it a swirl of fallen leaves that danced in its wake. Finn's thoughts drifted to the murderer. The killer's meticulous planning and twisted purpose weighed heavily on his mind, urging him onward.

Amelia's hand brushed against his arm subtly, a silent reassurance amidst the bustling chaos surrounding them. Finn met her gaze, finding solace in her unwavering support as they delved deeper into the heart of London's mysteries.

"We only have one lead now," Amelia said with a sigh.

"Tim Nolan," Finn agreed. "If he did send cryptic messages to Emily Stanton, it's possible he is our poetic killer."

"Or one of them," Amelia said, gravely.

***

The evening sun cast an eerie glow on the unkempt hedges and wild ivy that clung to the desolate Victorian mansion. Soon it would be dark, and that was not something Finn was looking forward to. Finn's sharp gaze swept over the boarded windows, noting how they seemed to stare back like dark, unblinking eyes. Amelia walked beside him, her hand resting lightly on the service weapon at her hip.

"Why does everyone have to live in a creepy location in this case?" Amelia murmured, her voice barely more than a whisper against the haunting silence surrounding the Nolan estate.

"It wouldn't be fun otherwise," Finn replied, his mind racing with the implications of what they might find inside. He had seen enough in his career to know that houses like these often bore witness to the darkest corners of the human psyche.

They reached the weathered front door, where peeling paint hung like ancient parchment. Finn raised his hand and knocked firmly, the sound hollow against the thick wood.

"Tim Nolan!" he called out. "Open up! It's the police."

Silence answered them – as heavy and unyielding as the door before them.

"Maybe he's not home," Amelia suggested, but her tone betrayed her doubt.

"Maybe," Finn agreed, though his instinct whispered otherwise.

Finn pressed his ear against the door. Barely audible, but it was there—the sound of someone or something moving around inside.

"You hear anything?" Amelia asked, quiety.

"Someone's in there," Finn answered. "Let's proceed carefully." His fingers twitched for the presence of a gun that wasn't there.

They exchanged a nod. With no further words needed, Finn turned the door handle and was surprised to find it unlocked. The door groaned on its hinges, a sound that seemed too loud in the quiet neighborhood.

The musty scent of disuse wafted out to greet them, and dust motes danced in the beam of light that cut through the gloom of the house's interior. They stepped into the threshold, their senses heightened, every nerve attuned to the possibility of danger.

"Clear left," Amelia said, her voice low but carrying in the oppressive atmosphere of the mansion.

"Right," Finn confirmed, moving in the opposite direction. His footsteps were near silent, a testament to years spent pursuing suspects through less-than-hospitable environments.

Adrenaline coursed through Finn's veins, sharpening his focus.

"Amelia," he whispered into his radio, the device a lifeline between them in the sprawling house. "Anything?"

"Negative," came the terse reply. "Keep your eyes open, Finn. This place feels... off."

"Understood," he responded, but as the words left his mouth, another sound broke through the stillness, guiding him with grim certainty towards the heart of Tim Nolan's secrets.

Finn's gaze swept over the chaos of the once grand foyer, the air thick with dust and the heavy silence of abandonment. The Victorian mansion, a relic of opulence now surrendered to decay, seemed almost resentful of their intrusion.

"Amelia," he whispered into the radio, his voice steady despite the eerie setting. "Take upstairs. I'll cover the ground floor."

"Got it," Amelia answered, her footsteps muffled by the thick carpet as she ascended the staircase.

Finn moved through the rooms methodically, his eyes scanning for any sign of Tim Nolan or clues to his macabre obsession. The trail of destruction was palpable, furniture upended as if in a desperate search, or perhaps the aftermath of a struggle. Pages torn from books and strewn across the floor fluttered like injured birds in the breeze that slipped through the cracks of the boarded windows.

"Looks like Nolan's been looking for something," Finn muttered to himself, bending to pick up a paper embellished with what appeared to be a complex diagram, its edges frayed and yellowing. He slid it into an evidence bag, a silent promise to examine it later.

Amelia's footsteps sounded upstairs. "Finn! I found him!"

Finn made his way to join her quickly toward a paint-flecked door, the heart of Nolan's madness, where Amelia had found him. The door creaked open to reveal a room shrouded in shadows, cluttered with artifacts of a bygone era. Amidst the disarray, Amelia stood still, her hands open clearly adopting nonthreatening body language, her attention fixed on the figure hunched over a desk.

"Tim Nolan," she announced, her voice clear and authoritative, though Finn could detect the undercurrent of curiosity that drove her every pursuit of justice.

Tim Nolan sat at a weathered desk, his figure a study in contrasts against the dimly lit room. Strangely, he wore an immaculate suit among the clutter, as though it were one final piece of himself that had not shattered yet. The flickering light from a lone candle cast dancing shadows on his face, accentuating the deep lines etched by sleepless nights and relentless pursuit.

His hands, normally steady and precise, trembled slightly as they hovered over a collection of yellowed papers spread before him. The intensity of his gaze was unsettling, piercing through the gloom with an almost manic focus. Strands of hair fell across his forehead, his eyes hinted at a mind consumed by turmoil.

The air around him crackled with an energy that seemed to emanate from within, an aura of desperation mingled with determination. Tim Nolan's expression spoke of madness tempered by fleeting moments of clarity, as if he teetered on the edge of revelation and ruin.

Nolan didn't respond, his hand moving frenetically across the pages of a notebook, as if trying to outrun time itself. Finn approached cautiously, noting the walls adorned with maps and diagrams, each meticulously detailed and eerily reminiscent of the industrial revolution's ingenuity.

"Mr. Nolan," Finn tried, softer but insistent, "we need to talk about your... projects. We're not here to hurt you."

The man looked up, his gaze momentarily locking with Finn's before returning to his scribbles. Around them, the room seemed to close in, the very air charged with the energy of Nolan's delusion.

"Look at this," Amelia whispered, nodding toward the wall where a large, intricate blueprint commanded attention. It depicted a Victorian factory, its architecture exact, its purpose ominous in its complexity.

"Working on something, Nolan?" Finn inquired, stepping closer to inspect the drawing. Each line spoke of precision, a plan devised with a singular, terrifying vision.

"Everything in its place," Nolan murmured, his voice barely above a whisper, yet carrying the weight of conviction. "Just as it should be."

"This wouldn't have anything to do with Luc Henshaw and Emily Stanton, would it?" Finn prodded.

The man grinned.

"If I didn't know better, I'd say this was the heart of your operation," Amelia said, circling the desk to stand beside Finn. Her investigative mind was piecing together the puzzle, the implications of Nolan's actions painting a grim picture.

"Or just the beginning," Finn added, his thoughts racing ahead to the implications of what the blueprint might represent. There was a connection here, a link between Nolan's fervor and the series of killings that had brought them to this forsaken house.

"Am I under arrest?" Nolan asked.

Finn noticed that the man glanced at a side door nervously for a moment.

There's something in there, Finn thought.

"No, you're not under arrest," answered Amelia. "But you are a person of interest in the murder of Emily Stanton."

"If I am not under arrest, then I must ask you to leave," Nolan sniped.

"Why were you sending threatening messages to Emily Stanton?" Finn asked.

"I don't have to answer any of your questions. Get out!"

Finn winked at Amelia.

"Inspector Winters, I thought I heard something moving around," Finn said, loudly. "Given we're chasing a serial killer, and we have evidence that Mr Nolan had threatened one of the victims, I'm *terribly* concerned that the noise I just heard is a possible third victim tied up somewhere."

"Well," Amelia answered. "If you believe an active crime is taking place, then that would allow you to legally search this place."

Finn's suspicions heightened as he eyed the side door, a flicker of movement catching his attention. Nolan, sensing their intent, grew visibly agitated and blocked Finn's path.

"Why won't you just leave?" Nolan's voice cracked with frustration, his eyes wild with defiance.

Finn noticed a slight limp in Nolan's gait, a detail that added to the man's air of desperation. Ignoring the protest, Finn pressed on, his gaze unwavering.

"Tell me, were you at a Victorian house in Bingham today?" Finn's tone brooked no argument.

Nolan's face contorted with anger. "No! I've never been there!"

In a sudden burst of aggression, Nolan lunged forward and grabbed Finn's arm, where the stitches from his recent injuries lay hidden beneath his shirt. Pain shot through Finn, his muscles tensing involuntarily as he winced.

Reacting on instinct, Finn swiftly twisted out of Nolan's grasp and expertly brought him to the ground with a controlled force. The room echoed with the impact as Amelia swiftly moved in to secure Nolan in handcuffs.

The scuffle had ended as quickly as it began, leaving Nolan subdued on the floor while Finn steadied himself, his jaw clenched against the lingering ache. Amelia stood by his side, her stance firm and unwavering as she ensured that justice would prevail in this tangled web of mystery and danger.

"What are you hiding in here?" Finn asked.

"Don't go in there! It's private!" Nolan yelped.

Finn turned and opened the door, stepping inside. The air thick with the scent of wax and decay. He moved cautiously, all the while wondering if Nolan had an accomplice nearby. Dust motes danced in the sporadic shafts of light that pierced the gloom.

A glint caught Finn's eye as he neared another narrow doorway, hidden behind a tattered curtain. Heart pounding, he pushed it aside and stepped into a space that felt like a sanctum frozen in time.

The room was dimly lit by candles that cast an eerie glow over the walls. A shrine dominated the far end, a statue dedicated to Ezra Bellamy. Finn's gaze swept over the display: old photographs with eyes that seemed to follow him, a large brass-handled knife that gleamed ominously, reflecting the flickering candlelight.

And there, presiding over it all, hung a portrait of Bellamy himself, faded but austere, his gaze stern and unyielding. The founder of this madness, thought Finn, his mind trying to reconcile the past with the present horror.

Amelia followed. "I've cuffed Nolan to a radiator."

"Bellamy's looking right at me. Seems Nolan isn't just a fan," Finn said.

"Understatement of the year," Amelia muttered under her breath, looking at the statue and painting.

Finn approached the shrine, the details growing more macabre up close. Among the homage, handwritten notes scrawled with frantic energy hinted at rituals, at a devotion that went beyond obsession. Finn's detective instincts screamed that this was the breeding ground for Nolan's unraveling psyche—a descent marked by each flickering candle.

"Look at this painting," Amelia said, pointing to a portrait of a man standing over a large crate. On the crate were the words "the heart of the machine" in clear writing.

"Amelia, Nolan's built a shrine to Bellamy down here," Finn reported, his voice steady despite the chill crawling up his spine. "It's like he's worshiping the guy. What the hell is the heart of the machine?"

"Look!" Amelia said, standing over a desk.

Finn rushed to her side. On the desk was an old map. Finn's fingers traced the edges of the map, the dim light from his flashlight casting an eerie glow on the patchwork of streets and alleys. The city of London sprawled before him in ink and paper, a labyrinth of history and modernity. His gaze sharpened as he took in the marked locations—two of which stood out more than the others.

"The old mill where Lucas Henshaw was murdered…" Finn started.

"And the bathhouse where Emily Stanton was killed," Amelia finished. "but what are these other locations?"

"I don't know," Finn said. "But we now have a suspect in our custody to ask."

CHAPTER ELEVEN

Finn sat across from Tim Nolan in the stark interview room at Hertfordshire Constabulary, the air heavy with tension. Amelia's presence beside him offered a silent reassurance as they prepared to delve into the depths of Nolan's twisted mind.

The solicitor, a middle-aged man with a stern expression named Paulson, sat next to Nolan, his pen poised over a legal pad. Finn noted how Nolan's eyes darted around the room, his hands fidgeting nervously in his lap. The man exuded an air of defiance that Finn found both intriguing and unsettling.

"Mr. Nolan," Finn began, his voice steady and probing. "You've been linked to both Emily Stanton and Lucas Henshaw through various means. Care to explain your connection to them?"

Nolan's lips curled into a sardonic smile, his gaze locking onto Finn's with an intensity that sent a shiver down Finn's spine. "I have no obligation to entertain baseless accusations," he retorted, his tone laced with arrogance.

Finn's gaze remained fixed on Tim Nolan, his expression unreadable yet piercing. The solicitor, Paulson, cleared his throat, breaking the tense silence that enveloped the room. His voice was measured as he addressed Finn and Amelia.

"Detective Wright, could you please elaborate on the alleged connections between my client and the victims in question?" Paulson's tone carried a hint of skepticism, his eyes flickering between Finn and Amelia.

Finn leaned forward slightly, his hands clasped together on the table. "Mr. Nolan," he began, locking eyes with the defiant man across from him. "Our investigation has uncovered records of cryptic messages sent by you to Emily Stanton prior to her tragic demise."

Nolan's facade wavered for a moment, a flicker of unease crossing his features before he masked it with a practiced nonchalance. "I fail to see how private correspondence implicates me in any wrongdoing," he retorted, though a trace of uncertainty lingered in his voice.

Amelia interjected smoothly, her gaze unwavering. "Furthermore, Mr. Nolan, it has come to our attention that you share a peculiar fascination with Lucas Henshaw—a fascination that centers around an individual named Ezra Bellamy."

Nolan's mask slipped further at the mention of Bellamy's name, a shadow passing over his eyes before he composed himself once more. "Ezra Bellamy is merely a historical figure of interest," he replied curtly, though Finn detected a subtle tremor in his tone.

Finn continued with precision, each word calculated to unravel Nolan's facade. "Both Emily Stanton and Lucas Henshaw exhibited an unhealthy fixation on this enigmatic figure from the past—a fixation that seems to have drawn them into dangerous territory."

Finn's steely gaze bore into Nolan, a spark of defiance igniting within him. "Ezra Bellamy, a madman with weird ideas about time travel and Victorian contraptions. If he were alive today, he'd be nothing more than a deluded dreamer lost in his own fantasies," Finn remarked with a calculated edge.

Nolan's eyes blazed with an unexpected fervor as he leaned forward, his voice laced with reverence.

"Ezra Bellamy was a visionary, Detective Wright. His inventions could have revolutionized the world if only he had been given the chance to see them through," Nolan countered passionately.

With a hint of skepticism, Finn raised an eyebrow. "There's no tangible proof of that, Mr. Nolan. Just fanciful tales spun by those who idolize a man lost to history," Finn retorted coolly.

Nolan's expression softened slightly, his eyes distant as if recalling a long-forgotten tragedy. "You speak of history, Detective, but do you know the truth behind Ezra Bellamy's demise? He was not just forgotten; he was murdered by a mob of Luddites who feared his advancements would upend their way of life," Nolan revealed solemnly.

"Ezra Bellamy could have changed everything if only..." Nolan's voice trailed off wistfully before regaining its usual composure. "But alas, history is written by the victors who silenced his brilliance."

Amelia's gaze sharpened as she leaned forward, her voice cutting through the tension in the room like a blade. "Mr. Nolan, we have reason to believe that you and associates were attempting to recreate one of Ezra Bellamy's contraptions, specifically the Tempus Machine. Lucas Henshaw possessed a crucial component known as the Difference Engine, which we suspect led to his untimely demise at your hands."

Tim Nolan's laughter filled the room, a chilling sound that sent a shiver down Finn's spine. "You truly think I would resort to murder for a mere machine part? How quaint," Nolan scoffed, his eyes gleaming with an unsettling glint of amusement. "I am not a killer, Detective Winters. I am trying to save the world from itself."

Amelia's brow furrowed in disbelief at Nolan's brazen denial. "Save the world? By what means, Mr. Nolan? By orchestrating murders and delving into forbidden technologies?" Her words dripped with skepticism as she challenged him.

Nolan's expression remained unperturbed, his demeanor exuding an air of calculated confidence. "The world is on the brink of collapse, Detective Winters," he stated with an intensity that bordered on fervor. "Ezra Bellamy understood this truth and sought to transcend time itself to alter our course. I merely seek to continue his work, to unlock the secrets that can reshape our destiny."

Finn observed the exchange with a mix of fascination and wariness, noting the unwavering conviction in Nolan's words. Despite his calm facade, there was an underlying zeal burning within him that hinted at deeper motivations.

"I may be unconventional in my methods," Nolan continued, his tone measured yet fervent. "But rest assured, Detective Wright, Detective Winters—I am a visionary striving for a future beyond our current understanding."

Finn's gaze lingered on Nolan, assessing the man before him with a calculating intensity. "Mr. Nolan," Finn began, his voice measured yet probing, "given your unconventional beliefs and actions, do you have a history of psychiatric issues?"

Nolan's eyes flashed with indignation, his jaw tensing at the implied accusation. "Psychiatric issues?" he echoed, his tone laced with offense. "Just because my ideas diverge from the norm does not automatically classify me as mad, Detective Wright."

The air crackled with tension as Nolan's words hung in the stark interview room. His posture stiffened, a flicker of defiance glinting in his eyes as he squared his shoulders, refusing to be reduced to a mere stereotype.

Finn maintained his steady gaze, unfazed by Nolan's reaction but attuned to the subtle shifts in his demeanor. The solicitor beside Nolan observed the exchange with a watchful eye, ready to intervene if needed.

"Mr. Nolan," Finn continued evenly, "our concern lies in understanding the motivations behind your actions and beliefs. Your fervor for reshaping destiny raises questions that warrant exploration."

Nolan's facade remained resolute, a veneer of composure masking any underlying turmoil within him. "I am not defined by society's narrow perceptions," he asserted firmly. "My vision transcends conventional boundaries and challenges preconceived notions."

"Enough to kill for it?" Amelia asked.

Paulson, the solicitor, interjected with a steely resolve in his voice. "Detective Wright, it seems evident that you have no substantial evidence linking my client to these crimes. If this baseless interrogation persists, I will have no choice but to remove Mr. Nolan from this unwarranted scrutiny." His eyes bore into Finn, challenging him to provide concrete proof.

Finn's gaze shifted from Paulson to Tim Nolan, his expression inscrutable yet focused. With a deliberate pause, he leaned back slightly in his chair before fixing his penetrating stare on Nolan. "Mr. Nolan," Finn's voice cut through the tension like a blade, "where were you on January 19th? The night both Emily Stanton and Lucas Henshaw met their tragic ends." The question hung in the air, heavy with implication and expectation.

Nolan's mask of indifference faltered for the briefest moment, a flicker of uncertainty crossing his features before he regained his composure. His eyes met Finn's unwavering gaze as he replied with practiced nonchalance, "I believe I was attending a literary gathering at the Mayfair Library that evening—a rather mundane alibi for your dramatic accusations."

Amelia's sharp gaze locked onto Nolan, her skepticism palpable as she pressed further. "Can anyone corroborate your presence at this literary event?" Her tone held an edge of challenge as she awaited Nolan's response.

Nolan's demeanor remained composed as he coolly retorted, "I'm sure the esteemed guests and scholars in attendance can attest to my whereabouts if necessary." A hint of defiance lingered beneath his calm facade, a silent dare challenging Finn and Amelia to prove otherwise.

Finn observed Nolan closely, noting the subtle nuances in his body language and speech patterns. There was a calculated precision in Nolan's responses that hinted at meticulous preparation—a veneer of confidence masking deeper uncertainties lurking beneath the surface.

Amelia's gaze bore into Tim Nolan with unwavering intensity, her voice cutting through the tension in the room. "Mr. Nolan, why were you threatening Emily Stanton with those messages?" she demanded, her tone sharp and probing.

Nolan's expression softened slightly as he met Amelia's eyes, a glimmer of somber earnestness in his own. "Detective Winters, I wasn't trying to hurt her," he began, his voice tinged with a hint of sorrow. "I was trying to save her."

Finn couldn't help but interject with a touch of dry humor. "Save her from what? The perils of live streaming?" he quipped, a playful twinkle in his eye.

Nolan's composure faltered for a moment before a flash of frustration crossed his features. "It's not just about live streaming," he retorted sharply, his tone laced with urgency. "Modern technology has set us on a path to destruction."

The room fell into a heavy silence as Nolan continued, his words carrying an undercurrent of desperation. "Technology has seeped into every aspect of our lives, strangling us slowly without us even realizing it," he explained, his voice tinged with genuine concern.

Nolan's eyes flickered with memories as he spoke again, this time softer yet laden with emotion. "I messaged Emily because... because years ago I knew her," he confessed quietly. "And in my own way, I was trying to save her soul from the grip of this technological abyss."

Amelia's skepticism lingered in the air as she absorbed Nolan's words, her gaze unwavering despite the complexity of emotions swirling around them. Finn observed the exchange with a mix of curiosity and wariness, recognizing the depth of Nolan's convictions beneath his seemingly radical beliefs.

"Finn fixed his gaze on Tim Nolan, his voice measured yet probing. "Mr. Nolan, were you the one who introduced Emily to the idea of exploring Victorian-era technology?" he inquired.

Nolan's eyes met Finn's with a hint of resignation. "Yes, I did," he admitted quietly. "I lent her some reading materials, hoping to guide her towards a path away from modern technology and its pitfalls."

"Our team will be searching Emily's messages to confirm any of your story," Finn said, "just so you should know."

Amelia's brow furrowed as she delved further. "Did it anger you when she chose to incorporate Victorian tech into her live streams instead?"

70

Nolan's expression darkened slightly before he replied, "It wasn't anger, Detective Winters. It was disappointment that she didn't see the potential for change beyond mere entertainment."

With a steely resolve, Nolan asserted, "My alibi is sound. You should check it."

As Finn and Amelia stood up to leave, Finn paused at the door, turning back to face Nolan. "Just because you didn't kill Emily directly doesn't mean you aren't involved somehow," he stated firmly before exiting the room with Amelia in tow.

The weight of unspoken truths lingered in the air as they departed into the hallway outside.

Amelia glanced at Finn, her brow furrowed in contemplation. "You're really set on this more than one killer theory, aren't you? I will say... There's something... off about this whole situation," she admitted, her voice tinged with uncertainty.

Finn nodded, a flicker of intuition sparking in his eyes. "I can't shake the feeling that there's more to this than meets the eye, that there are others involved," he mused, his tone reflecting his gut instinct.

"I'll have someone check on Nolan's alibi," Amelia stated resolutely, tapping away on her phone. "But he seems pretty confident about it."

Before Finn could respond, Chief Rob Collins strode into the room with a grim expression etched on his features. The air seemed to thicken as the weight of his presence settled over them, casting a shadow of foreboding over the investigation.

Amelia greeted Chief Rob Collins with a casual "Hi, Chief," as he entered the room. Finn couldn't resist injecting some humor into the tense atmosphere.

"Rob, the last time I saw a face like that was when I accidentally broke your aunt's priceless Ming vase," he quipped, a mischievous glint in his eye.

Curiosity and concern mingled on Finn's face as he asked, "What's wrong, Rob?"

The chief's response sent a chill down Finn's spine. "There's been a sighting of Max Vilne," Rob announced gravely, his words hanging heavy in the air. "He was seen in London near the London Eye."

Finn felt his blood run cold at the mention of Vilne's name. The elusive and dangerous serial killer had resurfaced in their city, casting a shadow of fear over their already complex investigation.

Finn quickly shifted from their current case.

"We should head there immediately and look around," Finn suggested, his eyes reflecting a sense of urgency.

"We already have people on it, but if Vilne was spotted near the London Eye, he's long gone by now," Rob informed them solemnly.

"Still, we should check," Finn insisted, his determination unwavering.

Amelia interjected softly, her voice calm yet persuasive. "Finn, we still haven't confirmed Vilne's involvement beyond a shadow of a doubt. Our current case involves an active killer. If it isn't Vilne, then we could jeopardize lives if we focus on chasing him now."

Finn hesitated for a moment, torn between chasing down Vilne and prioritizing the safety of potential victims. Slowly nodding in agreement with Amelia's reasoning, he felt a surge of admiration for her unwavering dedication to their mission.

With a sense of resolve settling over him, Finn acknowledged Amelia's wisdom. "You're right. Let's stay focused on what matters most," he conceded, a newfound respect shining in his eyes as they turned back to the pressing case at hand.

CHAPTER TWELVE

The glow of the computer monitor bathed Rajiv Choudhary in a soft blue light, casting stark shadows across his determined face. His office was silent except for the rhythmic clacking of the keyboard as he coded late into the night. He was on the brink of finalizing something groundbreaking, a new algorithm that promised to revolutionize data compression and ripple through the technological world. It was his magnum opus, a culmination of sleepless nights and relentless dedication.

Despite the lateness of the hour, fatigue seemed a distant concept to Rajiv. The thrill of innovation pulsed through him like an electric current, propelling him forward. He paused only to brush a lock of hair from his forehead before diving back into the labyrinthine corridors of his code.

As the lines streamed across the screen, Rajiv's mind wandered to the journey that had led him here. From a precocious child tinkering with outdated computers in his parents' home in India, to the ambitious young man who boarded a plane to the UK with nothing but a scholarship and a dream. The transition hadn't been easy; the cultural shift was jarring, and the loneliness had been palpable. But Rajiv was driven by a vision, a belief that his work could make a tangible difference in the world.

He remembered the pride in his mother's eyes when he landed his first job at a prominent tech firm in London, her voice over the phone brimming with excitement. "You're going to change the world, beta," she had said. And perhaps she was right. Rajiv's algorithm had the potential to alter the digital landscape, to shrink the vastness of cyberspace into something more manageable, more efficient.

His rapid ascent in the industry had not gone unnoticed. Colleagues and competitors alike marveled at his ingenuity, his uncanny ability to foresee the curve of progress and stay ahead of it. Rajiv wasn't just making a name for himself; he was etching his legacy into the foundation of the tech world.

Yet, as the hours wore on and the office grew colder, a sense of unease crept into Rajiv's consciousness. Perhaps it was the weight of expectation pressing down on him, or maybe the eerie quiet that enveloped the building after hours. He shrugged off the discomfort, attributing it to the looming deadline and his own overworked imagination.

"Almost there," he muttered to himself, fingers flying across the keys. "Just a bit longer, and the world will never be the same."

Unbeknownst to Rajiv, as he sat immersed in his work, history's shadow loomed ominously overhead. The past, with its dark obsessions and twisted ideals, was reaching into the present, poised to claim Rajiv as part of a grand and terrible design.

The soft hum of Rajiv's computer was a lullaby to his concentration, the rhythmic clatter of keystrokes a testament to his dedication. The glow from multiple monitors cast a spectral ambiance over the room, an electronic aurora borealis flickering across his intent features. He leaned back for a moment, rubbing tired eyes that had seen too many sunsets and rises from this very chair.

Then, it sliced through the silence—a noise that didn't belong in the digital serenade of his late-night labor. A mechanical whirring, subtle but unmistakable, like the sound of gears not turned for centuries finding motion once again. Rajiv frowned, tilting his head slightly. It was probably just the cleaning staff—their vacuum cleaners had made similar sounds before—but this was different. It resonated with an odd familiarity that beckoned him from thoughts of algorithms and data streams.

"Probably nothing," he mumbled, but his curiosity, a trait that had led him from a childhood in India to the precipice of tech revolution in the UK, wouldn't let him dismiss it so easily.

He rose, joints protesting mildly, and stepped out into the hallway. The fluorescents flickered overhead, casting long shadows against the sterile walls. As his gaze traveled down the corridor, his breath hitched.

There, at the far end, stood a figure—an anachronism that seemed ripped from the pages of a Dickens novel. The figure was clad in Victorian attire, complete with a frock coat and a top hat shadowing its face, which was obscured by a gas mask. Its presence was as incongruous as a steam engine in a silicon chip factory.

Rajiv's heart thudded painfully against his ribs. The figure held something in one gloved hand—a brass device, its contours lost to the distance but its purpose unmistakably sinister by the eerie light it emitted, a ghostly glow that seemed alive with malevolent intention.

"Who are you?" Rajiv called out, his voice steady despite the adrenaline spiking through his veins. No answer came, only the continued whirring from the device, growing louder now, more insistent.

This was no ordinary intruder; this was the specter of an era long gone, wielding technology that seemed as out of place as its attire. Rajiv's mind raced—was this a prank? An elaborate threat? But the cold dread gripping his stomach told him this was no joke. This figure was danger incarnate, a harbinger of malice wrapped in antiquity.

As the figure began to move towards him, slow and deliberate, Rajiv's instincts screamed for him to act. The promise of his future, the algorithm that would change the world—it all meant nothing against the primal urge to survive. He needed to escape, to warn someone, but his legs felt rooted to the spot, transfixed by the surreal nightmare unfolding before him.

"Stay back!" he warned, his voice betraying a hint of fear now. The figure paused, its head tilting ever so slightly, as if considering him.

"Rajiv Choudhary," it said, its voice a distorted echo from behind the mask, "do you believe in destiny?"

"Destiny?" Rajiv repeated, confusion momentarily overriding his terror. "What do you want?"

"Progress requires sacrifice," the figure replied, its tone clinical, as if reciting a universal truth.

"Please, I don't understand," Rajiv pleaded, taking an involuntary step back.

But the figure advanced, relentless, the device in its hand pulsing with a rhythm that matched the quickening beat of Rajiv's heart. And then, with the inexorability of time itself, darkness descended upon him, an abyss from which there would be no return.

Rajiv threw a punch, but the killer easily batted it away. Then another, and another. Rajiv clawed and scratched, fighting with everything he had to get away from the man. But it was not enough.

The killer then struck.

He stood alone, the shadows clinging to him like a second skin as he watched Rajiv Choudhary's life bleed out onto the cold floor. The dim light flickered over the brass device implanted in Rajiv's chest, casting an otherworldly glow on the macabre scene.

CHAPTER THIRTEEN

Finn leaned back in his chair, the dim light from the desk lamp casting long shadows across his face. The room felt oppressively silent, save for the soft ticking of an old clock perched on a shelf—its rhythmic beat a mocking reminder of their race against time.

"Remind me again why we do this?" Amelia asked, her voice a quiet undercurrent in the stillness of the office.

"Because you can't bear to be without my sparkling wit," Finn replied, his gaze meeting hers. "Because if not us, then who?"

"Sometimes it feels like we're grinding ourselves down," she confessed, touching the plaster on her nose, her eyes reflecting a weariness that mirrored his own. "I dream about Victorian London now, Finn. Gas lamps and cobblestones. People in masks. I don't know if I see London the same way anymore."

"Haunting but meaningful," he said softly. "You know, I've always wanted to make a difference, Amelia. To leave something behind that's bigger than myself." He paused, contemplating the confession. "But I do sometimes think, will there be much left of me by the end?"

"Is that your fear then? That the cost might be too high?" She leaned forward, her elbows resting on the desk.

"Amelia, I—" Finn started, but the piercing ring of his mobile phone cut him off mid-sentence.

He cursed under his breath as he grabbed the device, seeing Rob's name flashing on the screen. "Wright," he answered tersely, all traces of the quiet moment vanishing.

"Another murder," Rob's voice came through, grim and urgent. "Near Lornpike train station. Young bloke named Rajiv Choudhary. App developer with a bright future ahead of him. He was found propped up… but we think he was murdered elsewhere."

"Details," Finn demanded, his heart sinking.

"Found dead in one of the carriages. Bullet wound, chest. Antique pistol lying next to him. This one's got your Victorian signature all over it. And Finn..." Rob hesitated.

"What is it?"

"Rajiv was an IT expert and was working on something big, he'd worked with the government before. Higher-ups are very worried. You and Winters need to get down here."

"Understood." Finn hung up, the gravity of the situation settling over him like a shroud.

"Another one?" Amelia's voice was tight with concern.

***

The night embraced them with a biting chill as Finn and Amelia arrived at the Victorian train station, its dilapidated framework casting a macabre silhouette against the moonlit sky. They moved swiftly, their breaths visible in the air, their steps echoing on the gravel as they approached the scene.

"Another Victorian location," Amelia murmured, her eyes scanning the Gothic spires of the station's roof.

"Give me modernity," Finn replied, his voice low as they ducked under the fluttering police tape and stepped into the abandoned carriage.

Inside, the scene was grotesque yet meticulously arranged. Rajiv Choudhary lay sprawled across the ornate carpet, the fabric pattern clashing with the modern cut of his clothing. An antique pistol rested by his side, as if discarded after performing its final, fatal act.

"Like Henshaw," Amelia noted, though her tone carried no surprise—just a weary resignation that they'd seen this grim performance before. "He's been posed."

"Victorian theme, again," Finn said, squatting beside the victim. "And like Lucas and Emily, he was involved in tech."

"I wonder if he had any interest in Ezra Bellamy?" Amelia queried.

"Let's see what our 'ghost of progress' left us this time." Finn's hand hovered above a corner of parchment pinned beneath the dead man's palm—a deliberate placement. He donned a pair of gloves before carefully extracting the note.

"Numbers, symbols... a cipher?" Amelia leaned over his shoulder, studying the cryptic scrawl.

"Could be. And look here," he pointed to a line scribbled at the bottom. "'Midnight approaches, darkness encroaches.' It's a threat, Amelia."

"He's building to something," she repeated thoughtfully. "This killer has a message, a manifesto even. But it's buried in riddles and old-world nostalgia."

"Which means we're not just hunting a murderer," Finn concluded, standing up and locking eyes with her, "we're up against an ideology. A dark reflection of the world Bellamy wanted. I wonder if we're dealing with a cult."

Finn's eyes were still locked on the evidence bag, cradling the note when a gentle tug on his sleeve jolted him back to the present. An elderly, weather-beaten face peered up at him, framed by a tangle of unkempt gray hair.

"Excuse me, sirs, ma'ams," the man's voice was hoarse, like gravel tumbling in a hollow drum. "I seen somethin' strange tonight."

"Who are you?" Finn asked, his tone softening as he noted the man's threadbare coat and the life-worn hands clutching a battered hat.

"Name's Thomas," he replied, shifting from foot to foot. "I stay 'round these parts. The old carriages make for good shelter, see?"

Amelia stepped forward, her voice carrying the same calm authority she exercised at crime scenes. "What did you see, Thomas?"

"Was a tall fella," Thomas began, his gaze distant as if replaying the vision. "All clothed in black, he was, with a long coat that swept the ground. And a white mask. Terrifying." He paused, swallowing hard. "Had this book with him, too. Big, it was, with fancy writing on it. Looked bloody important."

"Could you see his face?" Finn prodded gently, noting the details mentally.

"Dark as it was, no sir. But he carried himself all... high and mighty. Like he owned the place."

"Did he do anything unusual?" Amelia added, her notepad ready.

"Just stood there, lookin' at the trains. Then walked off toward the station, quiet as a cat on the prowl."

"Thank you, Thomas," Finn said. "You look cold, can we get you a tea or something?"

"That would be nice," he replied.

Finn nodded to a younger constable who was standing nearby. She quickly disappeared and then, a few minutes later, arrived with a hot tea for Thomas.

He sipped it slowly. "Ah hits the spot."

"Thomas," Finn started. "You mentioned seeing this figure more than once?"

"Right as rain, Detective. Always by the old spots, like the derelict theater off Milton Street. I reckon he fancies them places, or somethin' in 'em."

"Always with the book?" Amelia asked, her pen poised over her notebook.

"Every time. Clutched to his chest, like a miser with his last coin."

"Could you describe the book?" Finn leaned in, his mind piecing together fragments of information.

"Old-looking, like something out of Dickens," Thomas recalled, eyes narrowing in concentration. "Leather cover, I think. Thick as a brick and just as heavy, I'd wager."

"Anything else about him that stood out?" Finn asked.

"His walk," Thomas said after a moment's reflection. "Steady, like with purpose. Like he'd walk through walls to get things done."

"Thank you, Thomas. This is very helpful," Amelia assured him, closing her notepad. "You've done a good service today."

"Hope it does some good," Thomas muttered, staring down into his tea.

"Thomas, the constable here can take you to a shelter, if that would be convenient?" Finn said, his heart going out to the man.

"Thank you, my friend," the man smiled. "Yer a good one."

As the homeless man was escorted to where he could rest out of the elements for the night, Finn turned to Amelia, a furrow etching deep into his brow.

"Let's review the footage around those buildings Thomas mentioned," Amelia suggested, flipping through her notes. "Maybe our shadow has been caught on camera."

"Good idea," Finn agreed, standing up. "We're onto something, Amelia. I can feel it. I think he moves around here."

A forensics team member approached Finn and Amelia, a sense of urgency in their demeanor.

"Inspector," the woman began, holding up a clear evidence bag containing a small card with a fingerprint. "We got a match on the print found on the antique gun."

Finn's gaze sharpened. "Whose print is it?"

The forensics member hesitated for a moment before replying, "A woman named Maggie Beckett. The database info should be with you now."

Amelia's fingers flew over her phone screen as she swiftly accessed information. Her brow furrowed in concentration before she spoke up.

"I have the address. Maggie Beckett lives above her antiques store on Elmwood Street."

"I want the security footage from any local cameras," Finn said, turning to the forensics expert. "Send it to us when you have it. I want to see if our killer has been using these train lines to get about."

"Will do."

"As for us," Amelia said, turning to Finn. "We are about to go to another antiques store, aren't we?"

"I promise I won't let that distract me this time," Finn grinned.

CHAPTER FOURTEEN

The police car's tires whispered against the cobblestone as Finn and Amelia pulled up to the shadow-draped facade of Beckett's Antiques. The sign above the shop, embossed with gold lettering that had seen better days, creaked gently in the night breeze.

"Beckett's Antiques," Finn quipped with an arched brow. "The creativity is astounding."

Amelia cast a skeptical glance at the darkened windows. "Looks shut to me."

"Look up." Finn tilted his head towards the second floor, where a solitary light still burned. "Our magpie's still nesting."

They exited the car, the crisp night air carrying the scent of rain on its breath. Amelia approached the door, her footsteps confident and purposeful. Finn followed at her side, feeling the familiar itch of anticipation in his gut. They stood before the entrance; Amelia rapped sharply on the old wood, the sound echoing through the silence of the street.

"Police!" Amelia's voice was authoritative, slicing through the quiet. "We need to speak with Maggie Beckett!"

Finn's eyes flicked upwards just as the glow from above flickered and died, plunging the window into darkness. He turned to Amelia, his voice low and steady. "Looks like our bird has flown the coop."

Their banter faded into the background, the seriousness of their task settling like a cloak around their shoulders. Silence enveloped them once more, the mystery of the night stretching out like an unspoken challenge.

A rustle from the rear of the shop caught Finn's attention, and he motioned to Amelia. "Stay here in case she comes out front. If our friend is trying to slip away at the back, I'll make sure she doesn't get far."

He moved stealthily towards the alley that ran alongside Beckett's Antiques, his senses heightened. The musty scent of damp cobblestones filled his nostrils as he edged closer to the corner. A flicker of movement in his peripheral vision was all the warning he had before a bin lid came crashing down on the back of his head. Pain exploded in bright stars behind his eyes, and he crumpled to the ground with a grunt.

"Lying down on the job?" Amelia's voice dripped with sarcasm as she appeared above him, extending a hand to help him up.

"Thanks for the sympathy," Finn grumbled, clutching the throbbing spot on his head and accepting her aid. "Where is she?"

Ignoring the jab, his gaze snapped to the figure clambering over a wrought-iron garden fence. "There!" He pointed, pushing past the pain as he sprang into action, adrenaline spurring him forward.

They sprinted after the shadowy form of Maggie Beckett, her silhouette a ghostly blur against the moonlit gardens. Finn's breath came in ragged gasps, his focus tunneled on the fleeing woman. But each stride sent a jolt of agony through his forearm, the stitches from an earlier encounter pulling painfully. It was a stark reminder that even consultants hired by the Home Office weren't invincible.

"Pick up the pace, Finn!" Amelia called out, her own determination mirrored in the set of her jaw as she kept up the chase beside him.

"Easy for you to say," Finn panted, his arm screaming in protest. He pushed the discomfort aside, propelled by the knowledge that the key to the Victorian-obsessed killer's puzzle might be just ahead of them, in the grasp of the antique dealer who dealt in more than just dusty relics.

The chase spilled into the tangled maze of back gardens, Finn's boots slipping on dew-slicked grass. Hedges and fences blurred past as he pursued the erratic shadow of Maggie Beckett, his heart pounding in his ears. He could barely hear Amelia's footsteps behind him, the thud of their pursuit a stark contrast to the quiet night.

"Left!" he called out, anticipating Maggie's desperate bid for freedom. But as they burst onto the neon-lit street lined with pulsing nightclubs, the throng of partygoers swallowed up any sense of direction.

"Amelia!" Finn shouted, but his voice was lost amidst blaring music and drunken revelry. He scanned the crowd, catching only glimpses of Amelia's determined profile before she disappeared around a corner.

Alone now, Finn gritted his teeth, the raw pulse in his arm a relentless reminder of his vulnerability. Yet the urgency drove him on, weaving through the mass of bodies, senses on high alert for any sign of the antique dealer turned fugitive.

There—fleeting like a specter between the strobe lights—a wisp of auburn hair, a flash of desperation. Finn surged forward, elbowing past a cluster of oblivious clubbers. His stitches screamed against the movement, but the thought of losing Maggie to the anonymity of the night fueled his resolve.

"Stop! Police!" It was a futile attempt, lost in the cacophony that surrounded him, but then he was close enough — so close he could see the panic etched into her features.

With a final burst of energy propelled by sheer will, Finn lunged, tackling Maggie to the wet pavement. The impact jarred his entire body, sent a fresh wave of pain searing through his arm, but he didn't let it slow him down.

"Gotcha," he grunted, pinning her struggling form beneath him. "Maggie Beckett, you're under arrest."

Finn's fingers fumbled for the handcuffs he'd attached to his belt, the metallic clink echoing strangely in his ears as he secured her wrists. For a moment, the world reduced to just the two of them, the chaos of the street a distant roar.

"Nice tackle," came a voice from above. Amelia. Out of breath but with a glint of satisfaction in her eyes. Finn exhaled, tension unwinding as backup arrived.

"Thanks," he replied, managing a grimace that was meant to be a smile. "I think... I need a minute. I must be getting old." And as he caught his breath, the figure of Maggie Beckett beneath him seemed far less significant than something he had just seen. Eyes watching him. The flash of a grin among the moving people around. It was a face all too familiar.

The face in the crowd he had failed to grasp.

Finn's knees ground into the wet pavement, his breaths coming in quick succession as he clicked the handcuffs closed around Maggie Beckett's wrists. His focus tunneled, the raucous din of nightlife pulsed at the edge of his consciousness, muffled like a drumbeat through thick walls. He looked up for a split second, sweeping his gaze across the crowd.

And there, amidst the blur of gyrating bodies and neon lights, was face again, features etched with malevolence. Max Vilne's smile sliced through the chaos, a haunting specter, standing there in the street. Finn's heart hammered; terror laced with anger constricted his chest. The image was fleeting, ephemeral, but it seared into Finn's mind like a brand. People walked by, masking him then from view.

"Amelia!" The urgency in his voice clawed its way out over the clamor.

"What?" she asked, noting the distress etched across Finn's features.

"Vilne," he gasped out, thrusting a finger toward where the ghostly grin had appeared. "There, in the crowd! Stay with Beckett!"

Without waiting for a response, Finn bolted upright, his stitches screaming in protest as he darted into the throng. His eyes darted from face to face, each one a potential mask for the killer who haunted their investigation.

"Stay with her!" he threw over his shoulder, not daring to see if Amelia listened. His senses stretched thin, seeking any sign of Vilne among the pulsating mass of revelers.

The scent of alcohol and sweat mingled in the air, the thump of bass vibrating through the ground beneath his feet. Finn shouldered past a group clad in glitter and leather, his vision tunneling as he spotted the familiar build of a man ahead. A coat that matched the right height, that same ominous aura.

"Vilne!" Finn's voice was lost in the music as he reached out, fingers curling around the man's shoulder, yanking him back.

The stranger spun, a look of bewilderment replacing what Finn had hoped would be Vilne's sneer. "What the—" The man's accent was local, his confusion genuine.

"Sorry," Finn muttered, releasing him. His gut twisted, doubt creeping in like fog over a moor. Had he seen Vilne at all? Was his mind playing cruel tricks, conjuring phantoms where there were none?

"Nothing," he whispered to himself, the bitter taste of uncertainty coating his tongue. "My apologies."

The night swallowed him whole, the chase leaving him empty-handed, with only the echo of a killer's smile lingering in his memory. A smile he could not be certain was real.

CHAPTER FIFTEEN

The sterile fluorescent lights of the corridor flickered intermittently, casting an eerie pall over the evening's proceedings. Finn leaned against the cold, unyielding wall outside the interview room, his fingers drumming a staccato rhythm on his thigh. Beside him, Amelia surveyed the door with a steely resolve that belied the concern tugging at the corners of her eyes.

"Think Beckett did it?" Rob's voice cut through the hum of silence, his gaze fixed on the one-way mirror.

Finn straightened, his hand instinctively reaching up to rub the tender spot on his temple where brick had met flesh earlier that day. "Her print was on the gun," he replied curtly, eyes narrowed in thought. "It's more than possible."

"You don't look well, Finn," Rob remarked, casting a sidelong glance at the consultant detective.

"Too many late nights," Finn dismissed with a wave of his hand, though the throbbing in his head suggested otherwise. Amelia's voice, soft but insistent, floated to his ears.

"I'm worried about you," she confessed.

"I'm fine," Finn grunted, more out of reflex than conviction.

"Something else on your mind?" Rob prodded, catching the shadow that crossed Finn's otherwise impassive features.

Max Vilne's elusive figure flashed in Finn's memory, a ghost at the edge of the chaos during Beckett's arrest. "Thought I saw Max Vilne," he muttered, unsure now if it had been a trick of his beleaguered mind.

"Are you sure?" Rob asked.

"No," Came Finn's quick reply.

"Let's say it was him, why would he be there?" Rob seemed willing to entertain the idea.

"At the tree back at the cottage," Finn reminded Rob. "We found an old pocket watch wedged in a hole of the trunk. I got someone to look at it and, at the very least, it was Victoria styled. This entire case seems to revolve around time and the Victorian era, it's too much of a coincidence. Vilne could be pulling the strings to taunt and punish me."

"I'll put the word out that he might be in the vicinity of the crime scenes. Maybe you should rest for a bit," Rob offered, but Finn's resolve hardened like diamond.

"No thanks. We see this through to the end."

With a collective breath, Finn and Amelia turned toward the interview room, its door swinging open with a creak of protest. Maggie Beckett stood defiantly inside, her posture rigid as the antique furniture she peddled. A storm brewed behind her eyes, the kind that had seen centuries of secrets traded for silver.

"Sit," Finn instructed, the word slicing through the tension.

Maggie's lips curled into a sneer. "I prefer to stand."

"Then I'll sit." Finn moved to claim the metal chair across from her, its legs scraping against the linoleum in protest. Amelia followed suit, her presence beside him both reassuring and unsettling, for he could feel the weight of her gaze on him, heavy with unspoken worry.

He could almost hear the cogs turning in her head, the way they might have in one of the mechanical contraptions from the past they were so used to piecing together—calculating, deducing, searching for the truth beneath the rust. But today, the machine in question was himself, and Finn wasn't sure he welcomed the scrutiny.

Finn leaned forward, elbows resting on the cold metal table, his gaze locked onto Maggie Beckett's defiant stance. Shadows danced across her features, etched by the harsh overhead light. "Ms. Beckett," he began, his voice carrying a razor-sharp edge, "are you acquainted with a Mr. Rajiv Choudhary?"

Her eyes narrowed, a flicker of confusion betraying her otherwise unyielding facade. "Why do you ask?" she countered, her tone laced with caution.

"Because," Amelia interjected, her words steady and clinical, "your fingerprints were found on the gun that ended his life."

Maggie's complexion paled, a stark contrast to the rich tapestries that hung behind her in the interrogation room—a touch of old-world charm in a sterile environment. "That's impossible," she gasped, her shock seeming to splinter the armor she had so meticulously crafted.

"Is it now?" Finn pressed, skeptically arching an eyebrow. "If you're as innocent as you claim, why did you run when we found you?"

Her lips parted, hesitating for a split second before the truth—or what appeared to be the truth—spilled out. "I've got a friend—she's undocumented—living with me. I thought... I thought you were after her, not me." Her voice wavered slightly, humanizing the statue of defiance she presented. "So I led you on a wild goose chase instead."

Amelia slid the evidence bag across the table with a practiced motion, its contents glinting under the harsh fluorescent light. The antique gun, an incongruous blend of old-world craftsmanship and modern violence, lay within, accusingly still.

"Recognize this?" she asked, her voice devoid of inflection yet carrying the weight of implication.

Maggie Beckett's gaze fixed on the bag, her eyes narrowing as if trying to pierce through the plastic and reclaim a piece of her past. "It's from my shop," she said evenly, her tone suggesting a mundane connection to an otherwise lethal object.

"Your prints are all over it," Finn interjected, watching Maggie closely. He knew the stress of interrogation often cracked the hardest facades. Hers was polished but not impenetrable.

"Of course, they are. I handle everything in there." Maggie's chin tilted up defiantly. "I can show you receipts, inventory lists. That gun was logged."

"Can you now?" Amelia prodded, raising an eyebrow.

"Absolutely." Despite the gravity of the situation, Maggie's response bordered on nonchalant. She sat back in her chair, arms crossed, a silent dare for them to challenge her further.

Finn felt a bead of irritation form at the base of his skull, a mixture of fatigue from too many late nights and the nagging doubt that had lodged itself there since the arrest. He leaned forward, his hands flat on the table, eyes locked onto Maggie's. "What about Max Vilne? Know him?"

"Never heard of him," Maggie replied, her facade uncracked.

Heat flushed Finn's face; he could feel Amelia's cautionary glance like a physical touch, urging restraint. But restraint was a luxury they couldn't afford—not with a killer whose identity slipped through their fingers like smoke.

"Easy, Finn," Amelia whispered beside him, her words barely audible.

Finn produced a photograph from the file and placed it before Maggie. The image of Max Vilne was grainy, captured from a distance, but unmistakably the man Finn believed was the puppeteer behind the chaos.

"Look again," Finn pressed, his voice harder than intended. "He might've been the one who bought that gun from you."

Recognition flickered across Maggie's features, a crack in her composure that widened just enough to let the truth seep out. "Him..." she breathed, a reluctant admission. "Yes, he bought the gun. Came into the shop couple weeks back, paid cash."

Finn's pulse quickened as pieces of the puzzle began to align, forming a picture that was as disturbing as it was incomplete. Max Vilne's shadow loomed large over the investigation, a specter Finn couldn't shake. And as much as he wanted to chase down that lead, exhaustion clawed at the edges of his consciousness, threatening to undermine his focus.

"Paid cash, you say?" Amelia jotted down notes, her pen scratching against paper in rhythmic bursts. "Interesting. Very few people deal in cash these days, especially for high-value items."

"Old habits die hard," Maggie quipped, but the lightheartedness didn't quite reach her eyes.

The room seemed to shrink, the walls pressing in as the significance of Maggie's recognition settled over them like a dense fog.

Finn's mind raced as he leaned forward, elbows on the table, scrutinizing Maggie Beckett with an intensity that belied his weariness. "The 19th and 21st of January," he began, voice steady but eyes unyielding, "where were you?"

Maggie shifted, her posture rigid, defiance etched into her features despite the vulnerability in her voice. "I was with a friend," she offered hesitantly, a tremor betraying her otherwise firm resolve. "Please, I can't—she's here without papers." The plea hung heavy in the room, a silent testament to her desperation.

"Without your friend stepping forward," Finn cautioned, standing up and pushing the chair back with a scrape that echoed off the sterile walls, "It doesn't look good for you, Maggie." His gaze lingered a moment longer than necessary, searching for some flicker of deceit or honesty before turning to leave.

Amelia followed suit, her measured steps a stark contrast to the turmoil swirling within Finn. They exited the interview room, silence enveloping them like a shroud until they reached the adjacent observation room where Rob awaited, his expression unreadable behind the reflective surface of the two-way mirror.

"Did you get all that?" Finn asked, eyes not leaving the mirror, half-expecting Maggie's reflection to reveal some hidden clue.

"Every word," Rob confirmed, his tone flat, the weight of procedure pressing down upon them.

"Vilne's involved," Finn asserted, the name tasting bitter on his tongue. "Facilitating this somehow."

"Right now, we've only got her word for it," Rob replied, skepticism lacing his words. "And without a solid alibi—"

"Trust me," Finn interjected, the memory of his pursuit of Vilne in America searing through the fog of fatigue. "Vilne manipulates. He pulls the strings and puts others in harm's way." His hands clenched involuntarily, the frustration palpable.

"Be that as it may," Rob said, meeting Finn's gaze with a steadiness that bordered on challenge, "without an alibi, we have no choice but to move against Beckett."

Finn's gaze lingered on the door through which Maggie Beckett had disappeared, her plea echoing in his mind. He turned to Rob, who was already preparing to leave the observation room, the weight of authority clear in his stance.

"Rob," Finn started, his voice steady despite the fatigue that clawed at him. "We need to consider giving Beckett's friend immunity."

Rob stopped mid-stride, a frown creasing his brow. "Immunity?"

"If she comes forward to vouch for Beckett's whereabouts during the murders," Finn clarified, leaning against the cold wall, feeling it leech into his bones. "But we'd need to check for reliability, it's possible the friend could make up the alibi. Either way, I think immunity might be worth it."

"That's not usual protocol, though," Rob said.

"But it is something the Home Office could do for us, isn't it?" Amelia added.

Rob mulled it over, his face a mask of contemplation. "Alright," he conceded with a nod, recognizing the logic in Finn's request. "But I want her statement first thing." With that, he strode out, leaving the room feeling suddenly larger, emptier.

In the sudden quiet, Amelia moved closer to Finn. Her hand reached up, her touch light as a whisper against his cheek, pulling his weary attention towards her. "That was very kind of you," she said, her voice a gentle murmur amidst the clamor of the day's events.

Finn offered a lopsided smile, the gesture not quite reaching his eyes. "Beckett deserves a fair shake if her alibi is true," he replied, trying to shrug off the heaviness that enveloped him.

Amelia studied him for a long moment, her concern evident even as she maintained her professional composure. "I think we should get some sleep," she suggested, her voice imbued with a soft firmness that brooked no argument.

"Sleep," Finn echoed, humor finding its way to the surface despite the gravity of their casework. He wanted to joke about Amelia joining him, but his tired brain stopped him from stepping over that seedy line. "Or we could go for a late-night date somewhere?"

The corners of Amelia's lips lifted into an amused smile as she headed for the door. "You wish," she tossed back over her shoulder as she exited.

Left alone, Finn let out a breath he hadn't realized he'd been holding, the shadows of the room creeping around him. Thoughts of the case, of Maggie Beckett and Max Vilne, spun through his mind like a carousel gaining speed, but he pushed them away for now. Sleep was calling, a siren song he couldn't ignore any longer.

CHAPTER SIXTEEN

Dampness clung to the air like a second skin, seeping into the very bones of anyone brave — or foolish — enough to tread these forgotten depths. The underground tunnel snaked beneath London's bustling lifeblood, a desolate artery where only shadows and vermin dared to dwell. The silence here was a living, breathing entity, punctuated only by the soft scuttling of rats. They darted between the tracks, their tiny hearts thrumming with a survival instinct that mirrored his own purposeful intent.

The killer's footsteps echoed, a steady rhythm against the rough-hewn walls, each step resonating with singular focus. His mind, a well-oiled machine, whirred with thoughts of the next kill. Anticipation tightened his muscles, yet outwardly he remained as calm as the stone that surrounded him. There was no room for emotion here — not fear, not excitement. Just the task at hand. Just the thirst that needed quenching.

Ahead, the dark maw of a shaft loomed. He approached, eyes adjusting to the abyss that beckoned him upward. With practiced ease, he scaled the rungs embedded in the wall, ascending from the bowels of the earth towards the night's canvas. The city's underbelly released him reluctantly, exhaling a breath as if expelling him from its secrets.

He emerged into a waste ground, an urban graveyard where the discarded and forgotten found their final resting place. The moon, a sliver of indifference in the sky, cast long, claw-like shadows that twisted amongst the rubble and detritus. A fence stood sentinel, its chain links a feeble barrier to the world beyond. He made quick work of the climb, his movements silent and assured, dropping down on the other side with a muted thud.

The outskirts of society unfolded before him. Here, amidst the cardboard kingdoms and tattered sleeping bags, London's homeless lay scattered like fallen leaves. They paid him no heed, too wrapped up in their own tales of woe and survival. Their faces were etched with life's hardships, each wrinkle a testament to battles fought and lost.

He moved among them, a specter unseen, weaving through the patchwork of human despair with a grace that belied his intentions.

They were all potential witnesses, but he knew they saw nothing. Invisibility was his ally in this place; it cloaked him just as effectively as the darkness did.

The killer's pulse thrummed with a rhythm that mirrored the frenetic heartbeat of the city itself. His anticipation was a living thing, coiled tight within his chest, ready to spring forth into glorious action. This kill would be a spectacle, one that would draw the consultant detective and his stoic Inspector into an ever-tightening web of intrigue. Henry Walsh, the unsuspecting streamer with a military buzz cut, would soon play his part in this grand design.

A quiet street corner unfolded before him, bathed in the sickly yellow of a solitary streetlamp. There stood his quarry, silhouetted against the dim glow, a figure of digital fame about to be snuffed out by hands that sculpted death. The killer's shadow merged with the darkness as he observed Walsh, who checked his watch with growing impatience. It was almost time.

The sudden vibration against his thigh broke the killer's deadly reverie. A message, its contents a leash tugging at his autonomy. Max Vilne's name flashed on the screen, a puppeteer pulling unseen strings. The text was succinct, a command disguised as a bargain: a message for Finn must accompany the body, or the final piece of the Tempus Engine would remain elusive.

"Damn you, Vilne," he thought, his mind seething with resentment. To be so close to the culmination of his work, only to have this meddler dictate terms—it was infuriating. Yet, he couldn't deny the thrill it added to the chase. The killer understood the stakes; the machine was the key, the nexus of past and future, where his brilliance would finally be recognized.

His fingers danced over the phone's keypad with deceptive calmness, replying in curt agreement to the demand. Securing the device back into his pocket, he stepped forward from the shadows, the giddiness replaced by a cold resolve. Henry Walsh turned at the sound of footsteps, his face a mixture of excitement and caution—a moth blissfully unaware of the flame it courted.

"Evening, Henry," the killer greeted, voice smooth like gravel underfoot. "I trust you haven't been waiting long."

"Long enough," Walsh replied, eyes darting around the deserted street. "This was your idea."

Walsh nodded, seemingly satisfied with the answer.

Silence reclaimed the alleyway as he stepped toward Henry Walsh, whose presence seemed almost trivial under the weight of the message just received.

"Risky business, meeting out here where prying eyes could spot us," Henry said, scanning the gloomy expanse of the backstreets.

"Risk is part of the allure," the killer replied, his voice a low hum in the cool air. "Do you have it?" Henry's question came like the soft tick of a clock—innocuous yet laced with anticipation.

"Hidden, where only the shadows can whisper its secrets," was the enigmatic response. Henry seemed to accept this, nodding with an eagerness that bordered on impatience.

"Let's not linger then," the killer suggested, leading the way. They moved together, two silhouettes against the dark tapestry of the London night.

The building loomed ahead, an old post office forsaken by time and progress. Its windows were soulless eyes, opaque with the grime of years neglected. Brickwork crumbled at the slightest touch, like dry bones turning to dust. As they stepped through the threshold, the silence deepened—a void punctuated only by the faint scuttle of vermin in the walls.

"Charming place," Henry commented, his voice betraying a hint of unease as he took in the decay.

"Charm is in the eye of the beholder," the killer mused, guiding Henry further into the bowels of the forsaken structure. The musty air hung thick with the scent of mildew and abandonment, embracing them with invisible, clammy fingers.

A broken counter loomed up ahead, once the heart of bustling transactions, now nothing more than a carcass of wood and faded paint. Tattered posters clung to the walls, their messages obscured by the relentless march of mildew and decay. Letters and packages lay strewn across the floor, undelivered missives that whispered of lives interrupted, connections severed.

"Quite the spot for privacy," Henry remarked, a nervous chuckle escaping his lips as he surveyed the desolate interior.

"Privacy," the killer echoed softly, his gaze lingering on the fractured glass that littered the ground, reflecting the scant light like fallen stars. "An increasingly rare commodity."

They ventured deeper, the air growing colder, as if the very spirit of the building disapproved of their intrusion. Shadows danced along the peripheries of their vision, cast by the feeble illumination of the moon spilling through the breaches in the architecture.

"Almost there," the killer assured Henry, his voice barely above a whisper. The sense of isolation was palpable, a living entity within these walls that had seen too much and spoken too little. Here, amid the forgotten remnants of the past, the killer felt a kinship—a shared understanding of being unseen, unappreciated, disconnected in the modern world.

Henry's voice quivered with a mix of anticipation and trepidation. "Where is the Tempus Engine?" he rasped, his eyes scanning the dilapidated corners of the old post office, as if expecting the relic to emerge from the shadows.

The killer, cloaked in the darkness that clung to the walls like a second skin, offered no response. Instead, a slight tilt of the head—a predator acknowledging the final plea of its prey—preceded action. In one fluid motion that belied a chilling grace, the killer turned on Henry, the glint of a blade catching the moonlight for a mere heartbeat before it sliced through the air.

There was a soft, wet sound, scarcely louder than a sigh. Henry's eyes widened, shock and realization dawning together in a silent scream as his hands flew instinctively to his throat. Crimson bloomed across his fingers, a stark contrast against the pallor of his flesh. His knees buckled. He crumpled to the floor, a puppet severed from its strings.

The killer watched dispassionately as the life ebbed from Henry's body, the pool of blood seeping into the cracks of the worn floorboards. There was neither satisfaction nor remorse in those cold, calculating eyes—only the acknowledgment of a task completed.

Swiftly, the killer stooped to drag the body, the sound of it scraping against the ground a harsh lullaby echoing through the hollow space. The corpse was positioned with an almost reverent care at an old postage weighing machine, the antique iron creaking under the unexpected burden.

A note was produced, its edges crisp in the killer's gloved hand. It was placed deliberately on the scales, a macabre balance between life's worth and words meant for another. The message for Finn Wright was simple, yet it carried the weight of a challenge, one that would draw him deeper into this deadly game.

"Like a nocturnal spy, return back home to the FBI," it beckoned, though ink and paper could not convey the taunting lilt that colored the killer's thoughts.

Retreating from the scene, the killer melted back into the night. With each step away from the old post office, the hope grew: hope that this kill, this message, would be the last required performance before Max Vilne upheld his end of the bargain. The killer vanished into the labyrinthine heart of London, leaving behind a fresh riddle etched in blood and shadow for Finn to unravel.

CHAPTER SEVENTEEN

Finn's sleep was a restless theater of shadows, the elusive figure of Max Vilne flitting through the crowd in his dreams, always just beyond reach. His head throbbed with the echo of the recent blow, and the line between reality and illusion had been smudged.

The sharp rapping at his door startled him into wakefulness, his heart lurching in his chest as if trying to escape the unease that clung to his subconscious. Groggy, he peeled himself from the tangled sheets, limbs heavy with a reluctance born from the disquiet of his dream.

Stumbling across the cold floorboards, Finn reached the window and thrust it open. The brisk night air stung his cheeks, pulling him further from the remnants of sleep. Below, Amelia stood, her silhouette etched by the silver glow of the moon, her eyes reflecting an urgency that knotted Finn's stomach.

"Amelia? What time is it?" His voice scratched, throat raw as if he'd been shouting in his sleep.

"I've been trying your phone for ages," she stated, her tone carrying the weight of unspoken news.

"Sorry," Finn mumbled, rubbing the heel of his hand into his eye. "I was dead to the world."

"Seems you needed it." There was a hint of concern in her voice that softened the edges of her authoritative demeanor.

"Ha," Finn scoffed out a dry chuckle, squinting down at her as he leaned on the windowsill. "This feels very Romeo and Juliet."

"Except you're Juliet, up there in the window," Amelia retorted, a wry smile touching her lips despite the situation.

"Touché, Inspector Winters," Finn replied with an attempt at lightness, though the jest faded quickly in the face of her grim expression.

"Get dressed," was all she said before turning away, leaving Finn haunted by the certainty that the nightmare he'd woken from had merely shifted into reality.

Finn's hand hovered over the staircase railing, a chill from the night air still clinging to his skin as he descended. He could hear Amelia pacing in the foyer below, the soft tap of her shoes against the wooden floorboards a stark contrast to the urgency that had pulled him from his bed.

"Amelia," he called out, his voice steadier than moments ago.

At the sound of his footsteps, she halted, turning to face him with an intensity that bordered on impatience. Finn reached the bottom step and met her gaze, the gravity in her eyes telegraphing the severity of what was to come.

"Tea? Coffee?" he offered, gesturing toward the dimly lit kitchen. It was a feeble attempt to inject some normalcy into the early hours of their impromptu meeting.

"No time," Amelia replied briskly, her hands clasped together as if to physically hold back the tide of information she was about to unleash. "Another person has been murdered."

The words hung heavily between them, a grim echo of the pattern they were becoming all too familiar with. The silence was brief, but it allowed the reality to sink its claws into Finn's already weary mind.

***

They arrived at the abandoned post office at daybreak, the building standing like a haunted relic amidst the silent street, a place forgotten by time but remembered by malice. Crime scene tape flapped weakly in the breeze, the only sound apart from their approaching footsteps.

"Inspector Winters, Finn," greeted Rob, emerging from the shadows that clung to the entrance. His expression was grim, his usual stoicism failing to mask the concern etched into his features.

"Chief," said Amelia, nodding.

"Rob," Finn said wearily, "what have we got?"

"Name's Henry Walsh," Rob said, leading them through the vacant corridors of the post office.

"Like Emily Stanton, Henry was a live streamer Big following. Millions in fact. This will be all over the news. He was only twenty-six."

"Damn," Finn muttered under his breath, his thoughts momentarily drifting to the youth snuffed out so callously, another life reduced to a statistic in their growing investigation.

"Here." Rob stopped short, and they rounded a corner into a room that once might have bustled with postal workers, now reduced to a tomb of scattered envelopes and dust.

"This is getting worse by the day," Rob commented, an understatement that resonated with the cold fact that they were now staring at a spree with no end in sight.

Amelia's rubbed her temples, a subtle sign of her rising frustration that Finn had come to recognize. He shared the sentiment, the weight of each victim pressing down on them, demanding an answer.

"Let's take a look," Finn said, stepping closer to the scene, his eyes scanning the environment that had become Henry Walsh's final stage.

Henry Walsh's body was a grotesque marionette, slumped over the tarnished brass of old postal scales. The grime of the abandoned post office clung to him as though he were part of its decay. Finn crouched beside him, the cut across his neck a violent contrast to the pallid skin, stark and deliberate.

"Clean," Amelia observed quietly from over Finn's shoulder, her voice steady despite the tableau before them. "No other bruises..."

"Means he knew his killer and was taken by surprise or..." Finn straightened up, surveying the desolation around them, "was forced here at gunpoint. No signs of a struggle."

"Voluntarily walking into your own death," she mused, with a note of irony that didn't quite mask her underlying horror. Their breaths formed wisps in the chill air, fleeting evidence of life amidst so much death.

At that moment, Rob approached, holding out an evidence bag that seemed almost insignificant compared to the scene. "This was left for you, Finn."

Finn's fingers closed around the plastic, his eyes locking onto the slip of paper within, a note that read: "Like a nocturnal spy, return back home to the FBI."

"Damn it," Finn murmured, his heart thudding in his chest. "He's directly involving me now."

"Could be a lucky guess, your identity, I mean," Amelia offered, but her tone lacked conviction.

"No," Finn said, his gaze still fixed on the mocking message, "this is personal." He could feel the threads of the case tangling, the killer's awareness of him a new complication in an already deceitful net.

"Vilne?" Amelia asked, her dark eyes searching Finn's face for confirmation.

"Yes," Finn replied, pocketing the evidence bag. But the doubt lingered, a nagging sensation that they were dealing with more than just one man's vendetta. A shiver ran down his spine that had little to do with the cold.

Finn's thoughts churned with the rhythm of his heartbeat, persistent and unyielding. As he stood over the body, the note's taunt echoed in his mind, an insidious whisper that promised no peace.

"Could be anyone who reads the tabloids," Amelia said, her voice slicing through the tense silence. "Your face has been plastered on every front page since this nightmare started."

"Sure, but Maggie Beckett pointed straight to Vilne when she sang," Finn countered, the pieces clicking together like clockwork in his head. The image of Vilne, a spectral figure in the crowd, seared into his memory from the day they'd cuffed Maggie. He rubbed the tender spot at the back of his skull — a painful souvenir from the altercation.

"Then why doubt it's just him?" Amelia pressed, her brows knitting as she scanned Finn's face for clues he hadn't voiced.

"Because Vilne is a beast, Amelia." Finn's voice was steady, but a flicker of frustration sparked behind his eyes. "The guy I grappled with wasn't as strong . Different build, different fighting style."

"Someone else," Rob interjected, his tone laced with the weight of realization. "How can you be sure?"

"Instinct," Finn replied, his gaze drifting back to Henry Walsh's lifeless form. "And fear. That masked man wasn't sure he could take me; Vilne never doubts himself. I doubt he'd wear a mask, either. It wasn't Maggie Beckett, as she was in custody during last night's kill."

"Two killers or more?" Amelia mused, the gravity of their situation settling over them like the dust motes dancing in the beams of the crime scene lights.

"Or maybe two pawns," Finn suggested, his mind racing ahead, "moved by the same hand… I want this to be over…"

Amelia placed a reassuring hand on Finn's shoulder, her touch grounding him in the midst of swirling frustration. "We'll get through this, Finn," she said softly, her eyes reflecting a steadfast resolve that matched his own.

As Finn's phone buzzed with an incoming call, he glanced at the screen to see Director Seward's name flashing. With a deep breath, he answered, "Director, isn't it the middle of the night where you are?"

"Finn," Seward's voice was calm and measured, a stark contrast to the chaos of their current case. "How are you?"

"I've been better, Sir," Finn replied. "How are you doing?"

"I wanted to inform you that the FBI higher-ups are reviewing your involvement in the Vilne case. A decision will be made soon regarding your status."

"You mean," Finn said, "that they've gotten sick and tired of waiting for the court case, that they want me out of the FBI, now?"

"We don't know that," Seward said, gently. "You know, there are a lot of us fighting your corner."

"I know, you've always had my back," Finn said.

"You've made quite a wave in the UK," Seward said. "Whatever happens, you should be proud of that."

Finn nodded grimly, steeling himself for the outcome. "And the court case for the damage to the hotel?"

Seward's reply was tinged with regret. "No updates on that front yet. The wheels turn slowly."

The mention of Vilne brought a shadow over their conversation as Seward continued, "Our colleagues at the Home Office have kept us informed about the Vilne case. Stay vigilant, Finn. The last time you stared him down..."

"He nearly killed me," Finn replied coldly.

"Just be careful, my friend."

"I will, Sir" Finn affirmed, his jaw set with determination. The weight of uncertainty hung heavy in the air between them as they exchanged parting words, each knowing that the looming decisions could alter Finn's path irrevocably.

"Are you okay, Finn?" Amelia's voice cut through the heavy silence, her concern palpable in the dimly lit post office.

Finn forced a reassuring smile, his words a facade to shield the storm brewing within him. "I'm fine, Amelia," he replied, though the weight of uncertainty bore down on him like an iron shroud.

Rob approached them, his expression grim yet determined. "Forensics is finishing up," he informed them, his tone carrying the gravity of their situation.

Finn's gaze swept over the desolate post office, each detail etched in his mind like a macabre painting. The stillness of death hung heavy in the air, a suffocating reminder of Henry Walsh's final moments. "He must have known his killer," Finn muttered, his voice cutting through the silence. "Either willingly walked into this or..."

Amelia's steady voice interrupted his thoughts, her practicality a grounding force amidst the grim scene.

"We should speak with his next of kin," she suggested, her eyes flickering with determination.

As if on cue, Rob stepped forward, his expression grave yet resolute. "His wife is Clara Redwood," he informed them, his words laden with significance. "She works at the Albert Victoria Museum."

Finn turned to Amelia, a flicker of realization crossing his features. "Victoria? That's a bit of a coincidence, considering we're looking for a killer with a Victorian obsession."

Amelia nodded in agreement, her gaze shifting to her watch as she noted the time. "It's 8:30 AM now," she stated calmly. "The museum will be opening soon."

"Then we need to speak to Clara Redwood and tell her that her husband is dead," Finn said, stoically.

Chapter Eighteen

The brisk London air did little to alleviate the tension knotting Finn's muscles as he and Amelia crossed the threshold of the Albert Victoria Museum. The grandeur of the Victorian architecture loomed above them, one of many tributes to the city's historical reverence, yet today it served as the backdrop for a grim task.

"Everywhere I look, I see Vilne's face," Finn murmured, scanning the ornate lobby for signs of unease or recognition among the staff and visitors. They all seemed blissfully ignorant of the tragedy that had unfolded mere hours ago.

"We'll get him," Amelia replied, her tone light but her gaze sharp as it darted through the crowd. The occasional banter between them was a thin veil over the seriousness of their work.

They found Clara Redwood in her office, a room cluttered with artifacts and the scent of aged paper. She had black hair, tied back firmly and dark brown eyes that seemed wiser than her years. She looked up from her desk, framed by bookshelves that groaned under the weight of leather-bound volumes, her eyes betraying nothing more than mild curiosity at their presence.

"Mrs. Redwood?" Finn began, his voice steady despite the leaden news he carried.

"Clara, please," she corrected, standing to greet them with a practiced smile that didn't reach her eyes.

"Clara," Finn acquiesced. "I'm afraid we have some distressing news. Your husband, Henry Walsh, was found dead last night."

Her reaction was a fleeting dance of emotions across her face—surprise flickered into existence before being swiftly replaced by a cool detachment. She sank back into her chair, her hands clasped tightly in her lap.

"Dead?" Her voice was steady, too steady for someone just learning of their spouse's demise. "That's awful."

Finn exchanged a glance with Amelia before pressing on, "You don't seem overly upset."

Clara's gaze met his, unwavering. "Should I put on a more convincing performance, Detective?"

"Most people would be distraught," Finn pointed out, noting the absence of tears or the expected tremble of shock in her words.

"Most people haven't lived my life," Clara said, a note of finality in her voice as though she'd closed the book on the subject.

Finn's instincts told him there was more beneath the surface, but the museum director's facade was as meticulous as the exhibits surrounding them. His gaze followed the precise lines of the Victorian dress Clara Redwood was examining, no doubt another piece for the museum to display.

"Clara," he began, his voice cutting through the silence that had settled between them, "how would you describe your relationship with Henry in recent years?"

"Separated," she said succinctly, as if the word were a scalpel cleanly severing any lingering emotional ties. "For two years now."

"Separated?" Amelia echoed, the question hanging between them as Finn processed the information.

"Indeed." Clara's eyes were steely, reflecting the museum's ambient lighting with a polished aloofness. "He wanted online adulation, I wanted a quiet life. Our marriage became... incompatible."

"You are still married. When did you change your name back?" Finn observed, the underlying inquiry evident in his tone.

"Redwood is my maiden name," Clara corrected, with a touch of pride. "I never needed Henry's. I always kept my own, even when we were together."

"Interesting," Finn murmured. He exchanged a brief look with Amelia and they shared a silent conversation. Was this separation the reason for Clara's lack of distress? Or was it simply a convenient truth?

"Clara," Finn continued, leaning forward slightly, "we're looking into a series of murders tied to someone with an acute interest in the

Victorian era. The killer seems to be fixated on ancient computers—Victorian relics. Henry is somehow caught up in it."

"Are you suggesting I have something to do with these crimes?" Clara's lips parted in a sardonic smile that didn't quite reach the cool detachment of her eyes. "Because I manage a museum?"

"We have to consider all angles," Amelia interjected smoothly, her tone professional yet probing.

"Detective, my passion lies in preserving history, not destroying lives," Clara retorted, her voice measured but edged with irritation. "I assure you, my involvement in the Victorian age ends at curation."

"Passion can be a powerful motive," Finn pointed out, watching her closely for any shift in demeanor, any crack in her composed exterior.

"Perhaps for some," Clara conceded, her posture relaxed but her eyes sharp. "But my interests are purely academic."

"Of course," Finn said, though the words were laced with skepticism. "Just doing our due diligence."

"Understood," Clara replied, rising from her seat with the fluid grace of another era. "Now, if there's nothing else, I have an exhibit to attend to."

"Mrs. Redwood," Finn began, noting the way Clara's hands stilled on the glass display case she was meticulously arranging, "where were you last night?"

"Here," she stated without hesitation, her eyes not meeting his. "Working on the new exhibit until the early hours. I often lose track of time among these antiquities."

"Can anyone corroborate that?" Amelia asked, skepticism thinly veiling her polite tone.

"I don't need anyone else for that," Clara replied curtly. She motioned for them to follow her through a winding corridor framed with Victorian portraits whose eyes seemed to follow them accusatorily.

They arrived at a nondescript door leading to the security room, where a bank of monitors glared in the dimness. A lone guard looked up, startled by their sudden entrance. Clara didn't waste a moment, stepping forward to log into the system with an efficiency that spoke of repetition.

"Here," she said, pulling up timestamped footage. On the screen, Clara appeared, immersed in her work, the clock above her head marking the ungodly hours. She fast-forwarded through it.

"Looks like you're telling the truth," Finn muttered, though his instincts told him something was still amiss. The footage was clear, showing her alone with the artifacts, but he couldn't shake the unease that gnawed at him.

"Does that satisfy your curiosity, detective?" Clara asked. She seemed to be putting on a cool front, but Finn detected something else underneath; an apprehension.

"For now," Finn conceded, giving Amelia a brief side glance that conveyed a silent conversation they had perfected over countless cases—a shared agreement that there was more to unearth here.

"Let's move on," Amelia said crisply, already heading towards the exit. Finn gave one last scrutinizing look at the monitor before following. They stepped back into the grand hall, where the morning light fought against the museum's perpetual dusk, casting long shadows that seemed to whisper secrets just beyond his grasp.

Amelia spoke again, her tone even but probing. "Ms. Redwood, are you familiar with an Ezra Bellamy?"

"Of course," Clara responded without hesitation, her fingers tracing the spine of a book bound in faded leather. "A Victorian inventor, quite ahead of his time. He believed technology had the potential to extend beyond its physical constraints—to influence the world like a force, supernatural almost."

Finn leaned forward, interest piqued by this new information. "What can you tell us about Bellamy's Tempus Machine? It's come up in our investigation."

"Ah," Clara said, a note of intrigue coloring her voice. But there was something else in her that Finn could sense, a fear mounting.

She glanced up from the book, her eyes flickering with the memory of countless texts she must have devoured. "The Tempus Machine was Bellamy's obsession—his intended magnum opus, though likely a dead end fueled by delusion. He claimed it could rewrite history, not in the metaphorical sense, but literally. An unfinished symphony of cogs and gears, never realized."

"Rewrite history?" Finn echoed, skepticism warring with curiosity within him. "How so?"

"Bellamy believed in a world unmarred by the Industrial Revolution—a return to simplicity. But he died before he could complete his work, leaving behind only cryptic schematics and wild speculation."

"Speculation that seems to have inspired a murderer," Finn muttered under his breath. Amelia shot him a quick glance, her eyes sharp with shared urgency.

"Right," Amelia said, filing away the information. "We believe Henry's murder may be connected to someone trying to build this Tempus Machine. Like some sort of time machine, as crazy as that sounds."

"The Tempus Machine?" Clara repeated, a slight shake of her head betraying her disbelief. "That's not a time machine, Inspector. It was Bellamy's vision of erasing the Industrial Revolution—returning us to simpler times, free from the shackles of technology."

Amelia leaned forward, skepticism plain on her face. "But is such a thing even possible? An actual machine?"

"Hardly," Clara scoffed, waving off the idea. "Bellamy was brilliant but eccentric. His Tempus Machine was little more than superstitious nonsense—a fantasy for those afraid of progress."

"Still," Finn mused aloud, "someone believes in it enough to kill for it."

"Perhaps," Clara conceded, her lips pressing into a thin line. "But you won't find your killer hiding among the relics in this museum."

"Maybe not," Amelia replied, her tone light but eyes sharp, "but we'll start by eliminating every possibility."

Finn's gaze lingered on the sprawling display of Victorian curiosities, his mind churning with the macabre dance of the past and present. The Albert Victoria Museum loomed as a testament to an era both grand and grotesque, its shadows deepening as dusk fell. Suddenly, like a lightning bolt, a thought struck him. Bellamy's machine, built to take down all technology... What if that were done today? How would it look?

"Think about this, Clara," Finn urged, his voice a low rumble. "If someone took Bellamy's Victorian concept and twisted it with today's technology... could they not create a virus to collapse the digital age?"

Clara, her face etched with lines of concentration beneath the austere lighting, paused and turned to him. "In theory," she admitted, her voice betraying a tremor of apprehension, "it's possible. A digital plague to send us spiraling back to gaslight and steam. It would fit in with Ezra Bellamy's desires."

"Terrifying thought," Amelia chimed in, her eyes scanning the surroundings—a habit born from too many surprises in dimly lit corners. "I hope to God that's not what our killer is really dealing in."

"Clara," Finn continued as they stepped out into a larger hall, the clamor of the public entering for the evening exhibition echoing off the walls. "Why would our Victorian enthusiast target Henry? What's the connection?"

Amelia's eyes were sharp, analytical. "Could Henry have known the killer? Maybe got too close to something?"

A flutter—an almost imperceptible shift—crossed Clara's features, like a ripple disturbing still water. Finn caught it, the faint glimmer of knowledge, or perhaps fear, that vanished as quickly as it appeared.

"Clara?" he pressed, locking eyes with her. He sensed the crack in her composed exterior, the hidden truths screaming to be set free.

"Clara," Finn said, his voice slicing through the murmured conversations and footsteps echoing off marble, "Henry's gone. But if there's anything left unsaid—any secret that might help us—you owe him that much."

Her eyes, pools reflecting the gaslight flicker of Victorian shadows, shimmered with unshed tears. "He...he wanted to make things right between us," Clara confessed, her voice a fragile whisper amidst the cacophony of the present. "He promised me a relic...something extraordinary for the museum. Said it would be the crowning glory of my collection."

"Who gave him that idea?" Finn probed, watching her face carefully.

"Someone he met," she breathed, her composure waning like twilight into dusk. "A man obsessed with the past..."

"Max Vilne?" Finn asked sharply.

Clara's nod was subtle yet laden with dread. She opened her mouth to speak, but at that moment, their reality fractured.

A dart, silent and swift as a shadow crossing the moon, pierced the air. It struck Clara's neck, and she crumpled like a marionette with severed strings. The poison acted fast—too fast.

"Clara!" Finn bellowed as he knelt beside her, his hands futilely searching for a pulse that was fading, then gone. His head whipped around, eyes scanning the crowd for any sign of the assailant—a glimpse of retreating malevolence—but the killer had vanished into the sea of oblivious spectators.

"Stay with her," he ordered Amelia, his voice a low growl of urgency.

Amelia nodded, her expression set in stone as she tended to Clara's lifeless form. Finn stood, every muscle taut, ready to give chase to a phantom that danced mockingly just beyond his grasp.

Finn's heart hammered against his ribs as he whipped around to seek out the assailant. Nothing but a blur of faces in the museum hall met his gaze. The crowd was a shifting tapestry, a mix of tourists and enthusiasts, none appearing more sinister than the next.

"I need backup at the Albert Victoria Museum, now!" His voice was terse as he keyed the radio clipped to his coat. "We've got an armed killer on the loose, possibly Max Vilne. And send an ambulance. We've got a poisoning."

"Roger that," crackled the response from dispatch.

Returning to where Clara lay, his steps slowed, the urgency giving way to an oppressive inevitability. Amelia crouched by Clara's side, her hands no longer fluttering with purpose but resting gently on the still woman's arm.

"She's gone, Finn," Amelia uttered, her words devoid of the warmth that usually colored them. Her professional mask was firmly in place, but the slight tremor in her voice betrayed her.

"Damn it," Finn muttered, scrubbing a hand over his face. He could feel the throb of the blow he'd taken earlier, a reminder of how close danger was. They were always one step behind, reacting instead of preventing.

"Did you see anyone?" Amelia asked, her gaze scanning the room as if she might find the answer etched into the ornate cornices.

"Nothing," he admitted with frustration, the word tasting bitter.

"Then we have to assume the killer is watching us." Amelia stood, her movements hinting at restrained anger. "They're mocking us, Finn. Killing right under our noses."

Finn nodded, his jaw set. "Let's secure the scene, get statements from everyone here. Someone must have seen something."

"Right." Amelia's eyes narrowed as she began issuing orders to the responding officers who were now flooding the scene.

Finn's heart clenched like a vise as he gazed down at Clara's lifeless form, the weight of guilt settling heavy on his shoulders. He saw her peaceful face, robbed of life too soon by a cruel twist of fate. The image seared into his mind, a stark reminder of the dangers lurking in the shadows they chased.

Amelia, ever perceptive to his inner turmoil, placed a comforting hand on Finn's shoulder. Her touch was a lifeline in the darkness that threatened to consume him. "It will be okay, Finn," she murmured softly, her voice a beacon of solace amidst the chaos.

Finn's jaw tightened, his gaze steely as he met Amelia's understanding eyes. "Nothing will be okay until Vilne is stopped once and for all," he declared with unwavering determination. The specter of Vilne loomed large in his mind, a malevolent force that needed to be eradicated to bring justice to those who had fallen.

Amelia squeezed his hand reassuringly before straightening up. "We need to search Clara Redwood's home for any clues," she suggested, her mind already racing ahead to the next lead in their relentless pursuit of truth.

Finn nodded grimly, the resolve hardening in his expression. "That's about all that's left to us now," he agreed, steeling himself for what might lie ahead.

CHAPTER NINETEEN

The afternoon had deepened its claim over the city when Finn and Amelia arrived at Clara Redwood's apartment, tucked away in a cobwebbed corner of London where the modern age seemed to have hesitated. The streetlamps began to cast long shadows on the ground under darkening skies, mimicking the bars of a jail cell—a fitting prelude to a search for truth among secrets.

"Charming place," Finn remarked dryly, his voice barely above a whisper, as they ascended the narrow staircase with steps that protested each footfall.

Amelia's reply was lost in her focus, her eyes already scanning for the unseen, the overlooked. Their footsteps halted before the door marked 3B, a nondescript wooden sentinel guarding the threshold to what they hoped would be answers.

Finn produced a key, courtesy of a quick stop at Clara's landlord's to collect what was needed after the coroner took Clara away. The lock gave way with reluctance as though aware of the invasion of privacy they were about to commit. They stepped into the gloom, the scent of aged paper and lavender greeting them, an olfactory epitaph to Clara's presence.

"Let's make it quick," Amelia said, her voice a stark contrast to the silence that enveloped the room. "We're not here to judge her decorating choices."

"Wouldn't dream of it," Finn replied, a hint of amusement in his tone despite the gravity of their task. He moved to the bookshelf crammed with volumes on Victorian history and ancient computing, his fingers grazing the spines as if coaxing secrets from them. Nothing.

Amelia sifted through a pile of mail stacked neatly on a hall table—a mix of bills and catalogs for antique auctions. Each piece discarded with a shake of her head; these were the mundane concerns of life, not the breadcrumbs of a murderer.

"If we don't find something…" she muttered, frustration nipping at her words.

"We have our skills," Finn countered, crouching to scan the lower shelves. His hand paused on a peculiarly out-of-place computer manual wedged between treatises on steam engines and social etiquette. Pulling it out, he flipped through pages expecting annotations or hidden notes. But like the rest, it held no revelations—just diagrams and technical jargon.

"Check her desk," Finn suggested, moving toward the window to let in some ambient streetlight. "Personal papers might give us something more... intimate."

Amelia approached the antique roll-top desk, its surface a landscape of old letters and photographs. She began examining each item with a methodical precision honed by years of police work. Yet, the search yielded little more than reminders of a life abruptly ended—a concert ticket stub, a faded postcard, grocery lists written in hurried script.

"Damn it," Finn swore under his breath. A sense of urgency gnawed at him—time was their most precious commodity, and it was slipping through their fingers like the dust motes dancing in the shafts of light.

"Keep looking," Amelia insisted, though her voice betrayed a trace of doubt. They were missing something, a vital piece obscured by the everyday veneer.

As they delved deeper into the remnants of Clara's existence, surrounded by the artifacts of her passions and pursuits, somewhere amidst the clutter of a life cut short—an answer whispering through the silence, was waiting to be heard.

Finn's fingers traced the edge of an old leather-bound ledger, his eyes scanning the faded entries for anything that might signal a deviation from the mundane. He was too seasoned to let hope rise unbidden, yet every nerve stood on alert for that elusive spark of connection. The room felt crowded with ghosts, the air thick with the residue of lives snuffed out.

"Mark had a thing for antiques," Amelia said suddenly, her voice slicing through the silence. She was sifting through a box of Clara's personal effects, her back to Finn. A sepia-toned photograph of a young couple—Clara and Henry, perhaps—lay discarded at her feet.

Amelia had very rarely spoken of her dead fiance in such casual terms. Finn didn't want to make a big deal out of it, but he knew that it was.

"Did he?" Finn asked, the ledger momentarily forgotten. He turned toward her, observing the set of her jaw, the way her fingers lingered on a small, intricate brooch.

"Pocket watches, silverware... even insisted on a gaslight chandelier in our flat." Her laugh was short, devoid of humor. "Said it was more authentic."

"Authenticity can be a cozy blanket in a cold digital age," Finn mused, leaning against the bookshelf that loomed like a sentinel over the room.

"Or a refuge," Amelia countered, dropping the brooch back into the box. She glanced at him, her expression unreadable in the half-light. "Either way, it doesn't stop bullets or poison darts."

"Neither does cynicism," Finn pointed out, pushing off the shelf to stand beside her. He could see the strain around her eyes, the toll of grief that never truly receded.

"Maybe not," she admitted, turning her attention to a stack of journals. "But after seeing Henry and now Clara..." She paused, a shiver running through her as if the temperature in the room had dropped several degrees. "You realize life doesn't wait for you to catch up. It just keeps moving until one day, you're the one who's stopped."

"Like a broken clock," Finn said, understanding the weight of her words. They both knew death wasn't selective or fair; it took without reason or rhyme. In their line of work, that truth was a constant companion, whispering in the dark corners of every crime scene, every hollow victory.

"Something like that," Amelia murmured, opening a journal only to close it again. Her gaze met his, steady yet tinged with a sadness that mirrored his own.

Finn skimmed through the faded pages of a leather-bound ledger, his eyes scanning for any hint of a pattern or anomaly that might lead them to the killer. The silence in Clara Redwood's apartment was thick, punctuated only by the soft rustle of Amelia turning over another fruitless page from her own pile of potential evidence. They were searching for something—anything—that could shine a light on the shadow that had taken Henry and Clara and left behind a trail of Victorian intrigue.

"Nothing," Amelia sighed, setting aside the last of the journals she was thumbing through. Her voice held a weary resignation, a sound all too familiar to Finn. He looked up at her, recognizing the fatigue etched into the lines of her face—a mirror of his own exhaustion.

"Amelia—" he began, but she cut him off with a gesture, her hand reaching out as if she were trying to grasp hold of an elusive truth that danced just beyond her fingertips.

"Finn," she said quietly, locking her gaze with his. "I've been thinking."

"About?" His question hung in the air between them, laden with unspoken understanding.

"Life," Amelia replied, her voice a whisper. "And how I've spent so much time chasing criminals that I've... I've neglected to live it." Her eyes searched his, deep pools of vulnerability that Finn felt himself drowning in.

"Amelia, you can't—"

"Please," she interjected softly, her fingers brushing against his arm. "Just listen. When Mark died, a part of me died with him. And now, seeing all this death around us, it's like waking up from a long, terrible dream. I think I've waited too long to start again."

Her confession hung heavy in the stillness of the room, a raw admission that stripped away the layers of professionalism and shared history between them. In that moment, Finn saw not the composed inspector, but the woman beneath—the one who had suffered loss and carried on, the one who stood unwavering in the face of darkness.

Without a word, he closed the distance between them, drawn by an invisible force stronger than reason or duty. His hands found her cheeks, cradling them gently as he leaned in, his lips meeting hers in a kiss that was both a balm for past wounds and a promise of solace in a world rife with uncertainty. It was a connection forged in the fires of shared grief and hardened by the relentless pursuit of justice.

For a heartbeat, or perhaps an eternity, they remained locked in the embrace, the chaos of their work forgotten. But reality would not be denied, and as they parted, the gravity of their quest settled back upon their shoulders like a mantle.

"Right," Amelia smiled, after a moment, her voice steady despite the tumult inside her. "We have a killer to catch."

Finn navigated the shadowed labyrinth of Clara Redwood's apartment with a forensic eye, his senses keenly tuned to the subtleties of disorder amidst the apparent normalcy. Each detail, from the precise arrangement of Victorian-era knick-knacks to the faint scent of jasmine that lingered in the air, was a potential breadcrumb on the path to unmasking a murderer.

"Diary," he mused aloud, breaking the silence that had settled between himself and Amelia since their charged moment. "If Clara chronicled her dealings, it could give us insight into her last days.

Something about the killer and their dealings with Henry. Anything would help."

Amelia nodded, her demeanor back to its usual sharp focus. The softness of their prior encounter seemed to dissolve into the shadows, replaced by the shared determination that always defined their partnership. She began a methodical search through the drawers of an antique writing desk, while Finn rummaged through the bookshelves, scanning titles and dates with a practiced eye.

"Check under the mattress, pillows," Finn suggested, sparing a glance at the neatly made bed, its covers undisturbed save for the indent of a head on one plump pillow.

"Got it," Amelia replied, her voice even but not devoid of the warmth that now underpinned their interactions.

She approached the bed, sliding her hands beneath the pillow with a careful precision honed by years on the force. Her fingers encountered the edge of a small, leather-bound volume, and she exhaled softly as she drew it out.

"Here." She held up the diary triumphantly, then flipped it open to a bookmarked page, her eyes scanning quickly.

"Anything?" Finn asked, joining her side, his curiosity piqued.

"Listen to this," Amelia's tone was tinged with urgency as she read aloud, "'Met with Chronos at Islewood Junction. Plans are progressing—'"

"Chronos?" Finn interjected. "Our poetic keeper of time."

"Islewood Junction," Amelia continued, her brow furrowed, "now, where have I heard that before?"

Amelia's fingers flew across the screen of her phone, the blue light illuminating her determined face as she scrolled through pages of historical data. The room was silent except for the occasional tap and swipe, echoing off the stark walls of Clara Redwood's now-empty apartment.

"Got something," Amelia announced without looking up. "Islewood Junction was part of an old underground rail network. Delivered post all over London. Shut down for decades, though. Wait... It probably ran near to the old post office where Henry was murdered, maybe even to where we found Rajiv's body!"

"Abandoned tunnels, again?" Finn remarked dryly, his mind already envisioning the cobwebbed shadows of forgotten passages. He had a nagging feeling that this case would uncover more than just dusty artifacts.

"Seems like we're destined to haunt the underbelly of the city," he added, offering a lopsided grin in Amelia's direction as they headed toward the door, urgency propelling their steps.

"Urban explorers or detectives, Finn?" Amelia quipped, pocketing her phone with a practiced ease. Her eyes, sharp and assessing, met his for a moment, sharing the thrill that came with the chase.

"Sometimes I wonder if there's much of a difference," Finn replied, pushing open the door and stepping into the cool night air. Shadows clung to the buildings, but their mission was clear: a beacon cutting through the uncertainty of darkness.

CHAPTER TWENTY

The wind cut through the empty streets, carrying a chill that seemed to whisper of secrets hidden deep beneath the city. Finn and Amelia moved with purpose, their breaths visible in the cold night air as they navigated the labyrinth of London's back alleys.

"Over here," Finn said, his keen eyes spotting the outline of a manhole cover partially obscured by refuse and years of neglect. He bent down, muscles tensing as he gripped the iron ring. With a grunt, it gave way, revealing a dark descent into the forgotten bowels of the city. His stitched forearm ached as it did so.

"Charming," Amelia quipped, shining her flashlight into the abyss. "After you, consultant detective."

Finn didn't miss the irony in her tone. He was often the one to take the lead, his peculiar insight into the minds of criminals giving them an edge. But this time, there was a hint of trepidation threading through his usual bravado. The idea of the killer, possibly even Chronos as a suspect, having predicted their movements, sent an uneasy shiver down his spine.

Without another word, Finn lowered himself into the hole, the sound of dripping water echoing up from below. Amelia followed, their descent into the darkness as silent as the grave.

The climb down was arduous, the rungs slick with grime and rust. When they finally reached the bottom, Finn took a moment to scan the area with his torch. They stood on the old platform of Islewood Station, a relic of Victorian engineering now nothing more than a haunt for rats and echoes.

"Which way?" Amelia asked, her voice steady but low, mindful of the oppressive silence that enveloped them.

"Tracks should be this way," Finn replied, nodding toward a tunnel mouth that yawned like an open wound in the earth. They trudged along the disused line, the beams from their torches catching on the occasional glint of metal or the scurry of vermin.

As they progressed, the unmistakable shapes of derelict carriages emerged from the darkness, lined up like slumbering beasts. Finn stepped into one of the carriages, the stale air smelling of decay and abandonment. His steps were cautious, alert to any sign of movement or danger.

"Looks like we're not the only visitors," Amelia observed, pointing to a set of fresh footprints in the dust. They exchanged a look, both understanding the ramifications. Chronos had been here before them.

"Keep your wits about you," Finn murmured, though he knew the advice was as much for himself as for Amelia. He brushed aside cobwebs as he ventured deeper into the row of ancient carriages, each one a potential hiding place for the enigmatic killer they hunted.

"They'll be writing about us in the papers again, Amelia," Finn said softly, his voice betraying none of the adrenaline that coursed through him. "Let's just hope it's not our obituary."

Amelia snorted, a brief spark of humor amidst the tension. "Always the optimist."

Finn's torchlight danced over a graffiti-tagged carriage, casting monstrous shadows on the peeling paint of its walls. The metallic scent of old rain and rust battled against the dankness of the underground as he stepped over shards of broken glass, his eyes narrowing at an anomaly amidst the decay.

"Amelia," he called over his shoulder, his voice barely above a whisper. "Over here."

A semicircle of laptops lay open like clam shells, their screens dark, their innards exposed and gutted. Finn's fingers hovered over the keyboards, not touching, reading the story of hasty deletion in the residue of dust that wasn't disturbed. He exchanged a glance with Amelia, her silhouette framed by the dim light filtering from the tunnel behind them.

"Chronos knew we'd come," he stated flatly, the realization sinking in. "It's all been cleaned out."

"Too clean," she agreed, stepping closer to inspect the scene. "He's been watching us."

Their search for clues was cut short by an eerie creaking sound that sent shivers down Finn's spine. And then, like a phantom emerging from the bowels of history itself, a figure cloaked in darkness appeared, its face obscured by a Victorian mask, grotesque with exaggerated features—a macabre nod to a bygone era.

"Show yourself!" Finn demanded, instinctively positioning himself between Amelia and the intruder.

The figure didn't respond. It turned and disappeared into another carriage. Finn gave chase, Amelia at his back. But as they flew through the next carriage, Finn saw it at the last moment—explosives.

"Amelia!" Finn screamed. He grabbed her and hurled both of them into the next carriage as the explosives detonated.

Debris and smoke plumed, and Amelia lay on top of Finn on the floor.

"That was close," Amelia said, gasping. "He set a trap."

"You can thank me later," Finn quipped, getting to his feet and helping Amelia up.

"I just need to sit for a moment," Amelia said, catching her breath, holding her side.

"Are you okay?" Finn asked, concerned.

"Fine, I just landed on the floor and..."

But there was no time to finish the conversation. The shadowy masked figure thrust towards them through the smoke. It lunged forward, silent as the grave, arms outstretched. Finn met the attack head-on, grappling with the assailant in the narrow confines of the carriage. Each punch thrown was a burst of pent-up frustration, each dodge a dance with death. The killer was strong, but Finn matched him move for move, fueled by the desperation to end this nightmare.

"Careful, Finn!" Amelia called out, her voice edged with concern as she searched for an opening to help.

But there was no room for two in this deadly tango. A sharp jolt of pain shot through Finn's rib cage as he took a hit, the impact echoing through the metal carcass of the train. He stumbled back, catching a glimpse of amusement flickering behind the mask's hollow eyes.

"Got your breath?" the killer taunted, voice muffled by the ornate facade. He drew back his cloak and reached for something lying on top of an old chair. It was a large blade.

Finn glared at it.

"I've got more than that," Finn spat back, regaining his footing. He feinted left before driving his fist towards the masked face, connecting with a satisfying crunch.

The killer staggered, momentarily off balance, but recovered with unnerving speed. The fight continued, a blur of motion within the derelict carriage, each strike a potential endgame, each block a stolen second of life.

"Chronos," Finn growled, the name bitter on his tongue. "This ends now. Where's Vilne!?"

Amelia lurched forward to help, but Chronos threw a kick, knocking her to the ground in a daze.

Despite the intensity of the battle, Finn's mind raced, piecing together the puzzle even as he fought for survival. The wiped laptops, the elaborate costume—it all pointed to a grand plan, one that Finn was determined to unravel.

The clatter of the fight echoed off the brick-lined tunnel as Finn, his breath coming in fiery gasps, scrambled up the side of a rust-eaten carriage. His hands grasped the cold metal edge of the roof, pulling his body upwards with a force born of desperation. The killer was relentless—a specter draped in the eerie stillness of the abandoned station, the Victorian face mask making them appear an apparition out of time.

"Amelia!" Finn shouted, but his voice was swallowed by the cavernous darkness. He threw himself onto the roof, the surface buckling under his weight. A silhouette against the dim light, the killer bounded after him, footsteps thundering like the trains that once roared through this desolate artery of the city.

Finn's heart raced, pounding a rhythm with the urgency of a Morse code distress signal. He rolled, dodging a vicious swipe. The killer's blade glinted—a whisper of silver in the gloom—and then pain exploded in Finn's shoulder, hot and sharp. The impact pitched him forward, his hand instinctively pressing against the wound, feeling the warm wetness of blood.

Finn reached out and smashed the killer in the throat with his fist. The killer reeled and looked around as if frightened by the fact that Finn would never stop.

"I might need your costume for next Halloween," Finn gritted his teeth, pushing through the haze of pain. No time for weakness—not when every second could mean another opportunity for the killer to murder.

With a feral grace, the killer seemed suddenly gripped by fear. He leaped from carriage to carriage, the old train cars groaning beneath their weight. Finn fought to keep pace, his vision blurring at the edges. He was losing ground, the killer always one step ahead, a twisted dance atop this graveyard of steel and glass.

"Chronos!" he called out, the name a challenge thrown into the void. But there was no answer, only the echo of his own voice and the relentless pursuit.

Just as the killer vaulted towards the last carriage, aiming for the gravel-strewn ground beyond, Finn lunged. His fingers caught the hem of Chronos' coat, gripping it with a desperation that surprised even himself. The fabric strained, the sound of tearing threads barely audible over the clamor of their struggle.

"Gotcha," Finn muttered, a surge of triumph rising within him. He yanked back, the killer's leg buckling, their balance compromised. For a moment, they teetered on the precipice—the brink between flight and fall.

"Give it up," he snarled, his own pain fueling his resolve. "End this madness!"

But Chronos was silent save for the heavy, measured breaths behind the mask, as if each exhale were an insult, a taunt, a defiance that Finn had yet to dissolve.

Finn's breath came in ragged gasps as he threw himself forward, his body crashing atop the masked figure. They hit the carriage roof with a thud that echoed through the hollow space below. With no time to waste, Finn's fingers scrabbled at the Victorian face mask, an anachronism that had haunted their investigation. The elastic gave way, and he pulled it off, revealing Chronos' identity.

Shock registered even through Finn's adrenaline-fueled haze. Staring back at him was not the face of some hardened criminal mastermind but that of a young man, seemingly no older than twenty-five. His features were sharp, almost delicate, with an air of arrogance etched into the lines of his face—a stark contrast to the brutality he had dealt. A cold smile curved his lips, as if amused by Finn's surprise.

"Too late, detective," Chronos taunted, his voice smooth and unnervingly calm. "The world will burn, and there's nothing you can do to stop it."

"Is The Tempus Machine just a virus then? Some cyber weapon?" Finn demanded, struggling to keep the killer pinned despite the stabbing pain in his shoulder.

Chronos laughed, the sound chillingly devoid of humor. "Using technology, Finn," he mocked. "To destroy technology."

Something in the man's eyes frightened Finn. It was that somewhere buried deep in the madness, Chronos believed in his words. He believed the world was about to come crashing down.

"Whatever you're planning," Finn said through gritted teeth, "it's over."

Chronos merely smiled wider, his gaze locked onto Finn's. "But detective, it's out of my hands. When I saw you coming, I passed all I have along to a mutual friend of ours."

Amelia's footsteps echoed as she caught up with Finn, who stood panting, his hand clutching his wounded shoulder, eyes locked on the young man beneath him. Chronos lay pinned, defiance still blazing in his eyes despite his captured state.

"Talk," Amelia demanded, her voice a blade of ice cutting through the tension. "The difference engine, the machine parts—what was it all for?"

Chronos' lips curled into a smirk that didn't quite reach his eyes. "You think this is all about old pieces of technology? Inspector Winters. Merely breadcrumbs to lead you astray." His gaze flicked to Finn. "You see, I couldn't allow Emily Stanton and Lucas Henshaw to get too close to The Tempus Machine. They were starting to understand what it actually was."

"Max Vilne," Finn interjected sharply, "was he the one behind the other murders? What was his role in all this?"

"Ah, Vilne," Chronos sighed, almost nostalgically. "He had something I needed—a piece of code from the black market. A vital component to complete The Tempus Machine." He shifted slightly under Finn's weight. "I did what I had to for that code. All he wanted was for me to lead you a merry dance"

"And innocent people died for that!?" Finn's voice growled.

Amelia exchanged a glance with Finn, both understanding the gravity of the revelation. It wasn't just about ancient technology; this was bigger, darker.

"Chronos, is the virus real?" Amelia asked.

"We'll know soon enough," Chronos said.

"Was it Rajiv Choudhary who helped create it?" Finn asked.

"In part," answered Chronos.

"We can't risk any of this being real. Vilne has the completed code now," Finn said, urgency lacing his tone as he pushed off Chronos to stand, wincing at the movement. "We need to find him before he acts on whatever plan you've set in motion. Where is he!?"

"Find him?" Chronos chuckled, shaking his head. "I've been nothing but a servant to his whims, detective. Where he is now, what he plans to do next—I'm as much in the dark as you are. I've played my part, and if he keeps his side of the bargain, the modern world will be brought to its knees."

Finn clenched his jaw, frustration boiling beneath his skin. Time was slipping away, and with Vilne out there, a shadow with the power to ignite chaos, they were racing against an unseen clock.

CHAPTER TWENTY ONE

The fluorescent buzz of the interview room light was a stark contrast to the darkness that had enveloped London streets just hours before. Finn's head throbbed from the blow he'd taken, a nagging reminder of the chase and the face that may or may not have been Max Vilne's, lurking in the periphery of the chaos.

Chronos sat across from them, hands folded on the cold steel table, his eyes steady and unblinking as they met Finn's gaze. The man's calm was unsettling, as if being in the custody of law enforcement was no more inconvenient than a delayed train.

"Mr. Chronos," began Amelia, her voice even, betraying none of the fatigue that had settled deep in her bones, "we can arrange for a solicitor if you—"

"I am no liar," Chronos interjected, his voice bearing a weight that seemed too heavy for the sterile room. "I've no need for legal shields."

Finn leaned forward, the movement deliberate, piercing the bubble of stillness Chronos carried with him. "Everyone's got a real name," Finn pressed, his tone carrying the subtle roughness of someone who had seen too many dark corners of human nature. "What's yours?"

"Names are chains of the past," Chronos replied, his voice laced with a conviction that bordered on fanaticism. "My essence, my true identity, is Chronos. I shed my given name long ago, like dead skin."

Amelia cast a glance at Finn, a silent exchange of skepticism. They knew identities could be obscured, but never truly discarded, not while threads of one's history clung to the fabric of reality.

Their suspect was an enigma, cloaked in the guise of an ancient deity, yet flesh and blood sat before them. Finn's mind raced through the details of the case, piecing together the strings that connected Chronos to the murders, to Victorian Britain, to the insidious threat of the Tempus Machine virus.

"Chronos," Finn stated, allowing the name to hang in the air, "time's up." His eyes held the other man's unwavering gaze, searching for a crack in the facade for the human beneath the myth.

Amelia slid a file across the table towards Chronos with a precision that matched her analytical mind. The paper's edge came to a halt just within reach of their suspect, its contents as revealing as the look of anticipation on her face.

"That's funny," she began, her words slicing through the tension, "because given your fingerprints, we were able to find you." Her finger tapped the file, a metronome counting down the seconds to his response.

Chronos's hand hovered over the dossier before snapping it open, his eyes scanning the contents. His stoic demeanor cracked, a fissure of anger breaking through the surface as he met the name staring up at him: Chris Harlow.

"According to this," Amelia continued, undeterred by the storm brewing in Chronos's eyes, "Chris Harlow was a lecturer at a small college in Kent." She paused, allowing each fact to sink in like weights into the depths of his conscience. "And that he disappeared 12 months ago."

The air in the room grew thick with unspoken accusations, the truth clawing its way out of the shadows. Finn watched the man across from them closely, every muscle twitch, every clench of the jaw. He saw not a mythological figure, but a man cornered by his past, haunted by the alias he'd crafted like a shield against the world.

Chronos sat back, his chair scraping against the floor, a sound that echoed the tumultuous turn of his thoughts. But Finn had seen enough, witnessed the momentary lapse, the ripple across an otherwise placid lake. Now, it was only a matter of time until they found the stone that caused it.

Finn leaned forward, his elbows resting on the cold metal table as he scrutinized the man known as Chronos. The sterile light of the interview room glinted off the handcuffs that bound their suspect to the reality he so desperately tried to escape.

"Names are just labels, ephemeral and without essence," Chronos declared, his voice a concoction of defiance and delusion. "I discarded mine for a cause far greater than most can comprehend."

Amelia's brow furrowed, her patience fraying like an overused rope. "A cause? You talk about sacrifice, but you left behind children. Was abandoning them part of your 'greater good'?"

He fixed her with a gaze that was meant to be unwavering but betrayed a flicker of conflict. "My children," he said slowly, as if tasting the unfamiliar words, "will inherit a world unshackled from the chains of technology once the Tempus Machine virus is released."

Finn observed the man's fervor, the way his hands animatedly sketched a future free from digital constraints. It was the passion of a believer, or perhaps the desperation of a dreamer. Finn's mind, however, lingered on the man's past rather than his prophesied future.

"Did you find solace in the past, Chris?" Finn prodded casually, using the name as a hook. "Was it comforting to retreat there when reality didn't match up to expectations?"

The color rose in Chronos's cheeks, a stark contrast to the clinical white walls surrounding them. His jaw tensed visibly, anger seeping through the cracks of his cultivated calm.

Finn pressed on, unfazed by the brewing storm. "There's a statement here that one of our constables took," he continued, tapping a finger on the stack of papers retrieved from their previous encounter with Chronos's ex-wife. "It says Chris Harlow was bullied badly as a child, so much so that she feared you had suffered a breakdown—a retreat into memories and old hurts."

Chronos's mouth twisted bitterly, the rawness of old wounds written across his face. But Finn knew better than to relent; this was the moment they could unravel the enigma before them.

"Is that why you want to erase technology, Chris?" Finn asked pointedly. "To wipe clean the slate of a world that's been nothing but cruel to you?"

The room held its breath, awaiting a confession that dangled precariously on the edge of revelation.

Finn studied Chronos, whose real name—Chris Harlow—seemed to have become a trigger for his buried traumas. The man's face was now shaded with the telltale signs of anger and vulnerability.

"Did you ever use the historical past as a sanctuary, Chris?" Finn asked, watching closely as the question landed like a jab to Chronos's ego. "I know that when I was a kid, if things got bad, I disappeared into detective fiction and old ghost story collections from decades ago. Part of me wanted to go back to when things seemed more easily defined. Villains were villains. Heroes were heroes. Even if it didn't hold up to scrutiny, it was enough to let me escape my childhood woes. Did you escape into history books, I wonder? All to escape a horrible past. Substituting it for a much older one. With no hope for the future, you could only look back. Not to your own past, that was too difficult. But to the Victorian era, where things made more sense to you through 21st century eyes."

The flush of red that spread across Chronos's cheeks was as revealing as an open book. It betrayed the truth without the need for words, but Finn needed more than silent admissions.

"Or are you brave enough to deal with the here and now, now that the mask is removed. Where is Vilne?" Finn's voice was firm, unyielding.

Chronos's eyes flashed defiantly. "I've told you before, I don't know," he spat out, the frustration in his voice growing with every syllable.

"Chris," Finn said. "Let me tell you what I see: I see a man who has lost his marriage, unable to attend to the scars of being bullied as a kid. Those scars had grown, but you had been able to hide them, at least until your marriage collapsed. With no loving wife to listen to you or help you through it, you turned inward, and when you did that you only found bitterness. A bitterness for the world, a world you wanted to punish. You killed people who you had some connection to through your project, people who had no idea what you were trying to build, but who could get you closer to it. And yet... You were manipulated by someone smarter than you, Max Vilne. He used your insecurities and hatred for the world against you, and your expertise in the past... He is the real mastermind. You are just a sheep."

"A sheep!?" Chris screamed. "I am a dreamweaver. I am Chronos! I killed with precision, and I helped bring all of this to fruition. You have no idea what's in store for you!"

Chris grinned. "Do you think those fools were killed because they were involved in our project? Some were... But some were dispatched simply to reel you in. You and your red-headed partner. So that the final dance can play out! You are the sheep! You've been solving crimes with no rhyme or reason, all designed to buy us time, time to bring the Tempus Machine online! I will say not a word more!"

Finn felt sick to his stomach. Chris wouldn't mention Vilne, but what he had said was enough to make Finn reach for a terrible conclusion—that Vilne had ordered the deaths just to give Finn something to chase.

"You might not want to give up Vilne," Finn said. "But let me promise you, neither of you will prevail. It'll all have been for nothing! Come on, Amelia." Finn motioned towards the door. They stepped into the quiet of the hallway where the tension from the interrogation room seemed to dissipate.

"Think there's any truth to it? A virus that could take down modern technology?" Amelia's question sliced through the silence.

Finn's mind raced with the possibilities. He knew what Vilne was capable of; the man was a ghost in the machine, elusive and dangerous. "No," he lied smoothly, unwilling to stoke her fears. "But there's still so much that doesn't make sense. Either way, we have to find Vilne."

Amelia sighed, her shoulders slumping slightly. "We've got no way to trace him."

"Let's leave it to the tech guys," Finn suggested pragmatically. "They might be able to extract something useful from Chronos's computers."

As they walked away, Finn felt the weight of uncertainty settle over him. The Tempus Machine was out there, and time, which seemed to be on Chronos's side, was running out for them.

The interrogation room's door clicked shut behind them, sealing away the enigma that was Chronos. Finn rubbed at his temple, feeling the echo of a headache born from a mix of exhaustion and the earlier blow to his head.

"Long day," he muttered, more to himself than to Amelia, who stood beside him, her gaze still fixed on the closed door as if she could see through it to the secrets beyond.

"Understatement," Amelia replied, her voice carrying a weariness that mirrored his own.

Finn glanced sideways at his partner. The fluorescent lights of the corridor cast harsh shadows across her face, accentuating the determination etched into her features—a resolute sculpture of duty and drive.

"You should head home," he said, his tone gentle yet laced with concern. "Get some rest."

"It doesn't feel like the time to take a break, Finn."

"What else can we do right now? The tech guys will be ready with their assessment in a couple of hours, other than that the trail is cold," Finn said. "We're exhausted, and the second the tech guys get anything from Chronos' files, we might have to work 24 hours round the clock to catch Vilne, if this computer virus is even a real thing. This is the calm before the storm. Use it to get some sleep."

Amelia turned to face him, her eyes holding his for a moment before she nodded slowly. "I will."

"Need a lift?" Finn offered, already picturing the silent cab ride where the day's events would replay over in their minds without need for words.

"No, thanks." She hesitated, then added, "There's something I need to do. Something overdue."

Finn's brows knitted together in curiosity. "What is it?"

A small smile tugged at the corners of Amelia's mouth. She reached out, her hand warm against his cheek—a brief, comforting touch. "Don't worry about it," she said softly, her eyes revealing nothing.

He watched her walk away, her figure retreating into the labyrinth of Hertfordshire Constabulary's dimly lit corridors.

CHAPTER TWENTY TWO

The moon hung low in the sky, casting a pallid glow over the sprawling cemetery. Amelia's footsteps crunched on the gravel path, the sound stark against the silence of the night. She navigated between the weathered headstones with a practiced ease, her senses tuned to the task at hand. This was a woman who spent her days piecing together puzzles hidden in the shadows of human nature, yet now she sought solace in the quiet company of the dead.

As she reached Mark's grave, Amelia came to a standstill. The cool breeze stirred the hem of her coat, but inside she felt numb. Here, under the indifferent gaze of the stars, the world seemed to slow down for a brief moment. She looked at the inscription on the headstone – Mark's name etched into the unyielding stone, the dates marking the all-too-short bookends of his life.

A deep breath helped steady her, though her heart continued its uneven rhythm. Her mind, always so adept at cutting through the noise and finding the truth, churned with a tumultuous mix of thoughts and memories. In the solitude of the graveyard, Amelia allowed herself this rare pause, a moment to let the facade of the unflappable Inspector Winters slip just slightly.

Before her, the headstone stood as a testament to what had been—a love lost to the cruel twist of fate. The professional mask she wore daily, the one that allowed her to stare down suspects and navigate the treacherous waters of high-profile murder cases, seemed out of place here. This was personal, intimate, and even though she was alone, vulnerability prickled at the edges of her composed exterior.

Amelia's eyes traced the letters of Mark's name, each one a stark reminder of promises unfulfilled and dreams shattered. Yet, even as grief tugged at her, the ember of determination that drove her every action refused to be extinguished. She had forged a path through darkness before and would do so again, alongside Finn, whose sharp wit and relentless pursuit of justice matched her own.

But tonight, she was not Detective Winters. Tonight, she was simply Amelia, standing before the memory of the man she'd planned to spend her life with, gathering the shards of her past as she prepared to speak words that weighed heavy on her soul.

Amelia exhaled a misty breath into the cold night air, her gaze not leaving the worn edges of the headstone. The cemetery was still, save for the rustling of autumn leaves that danced whimsically among the graves. She pressed her lips together, steeling herself for the confession that had been haunting the corners of her mind.

"Mark," she began, her voice no more than a whisper, yet it carried in the silence like a sacred vow. "I love you. Deeply. You're woven into the very fabric of who I am."

The words felt like stones in her mouth, heavy with truth and the burden of what came next. Amelia's fingers traced the cold granite before her, taking comfort in its unyielding presence.

"But there's something else, something I need to say." She paused, collecting her thoughts as if they were scattered pieces of a puzzle she was only now ready to solve. "I've found... someone. Finn Wright, my partner. He's infuriating at times, stubborn, too clever by half..."

She smiled faintly, the ghost of their banter flitting across her memory. It was a stark contrast to the solemnity of the graveyard, yet it was as much a part of her as the grief that clung to her soul.

"And I've fallen for him," Amelia admitted to the night, the admission liberating and agonizing all at once. "He understands the darkness we face every day, the monsters we chase. And he stands beside me, unwavering."

A shiver ran down her spine, not from the chill in the air but from the realization of how much she'd come to rely on Finn's presence. How his rare smiles could light up the dim corridors of Hertfordshire Constabulary, how his keen insight often unraveled the most intricate crimes.

"Mark, I want to let go of this guilt," she murmured, closing her eyes briefly as if to shut out the world and its judgments. "To embrace this new path without feeling like I'm betraying what we had."

Her hands clenched into fists at her sides, the fight within her rising. The same determination that propelled her through the twisted labyrinths of murder investigations was now fueling her resolve to accept happiness where she could find it.

"Because I know that's what you would want for me," she finished, her voice steady now, the tremor gone. Her heart was a tumult of emotion, but beneath it all lay a newfound clarity.

She gazed one last time at the grave that held so many of her lost dreams. Amelia stood in the stillness of the cemetery, her breath forming ghostly tendrils in the cold night air. The sense of solitude was palpable, wrapping around her like a shroud as she faced the stone sentinel of Mark's grave. She took a deep breath, the sharp scent of freshly turned earth and age-old stone filling her nostrils, steadying her nerves.

"Mark," she began, her voice barely above a whisper, "if there's some part of you out there... if you're listening, I need a sign." Her eyes searched the darkness, half-expecting to see an ethereal figure or feel a comforting touch. Anything to guide her through the twisting path of grief and longing that lay before her.

Silence was her only answer, save for the rustle of leaves in the gentle night breeze. It was the kind of quiet that could drive a person mad with its intensity, the kind that seemed to press down on your chest and demand your secrets.

Finn would have scoffed at such superstitions, Amelia mused. His logical mind dissected the world into evidence and deduction. Yet even he couldn't explain away the human need for connection, for a sign that they weren't alone in their struggles.

As she waited, the air grew colder, seeping into her bones. Then, a sudden movement caught her eye. Her gaze snapped to the left, where a shadow flitted between two headstones in the distance. Her heart hitched, the adrenaline rush all too familiar, like a siren call summoning her back to duty.

Amelia's hand instinctively clenched. Her practical mind urged caution, while her police training screamed for action. She strained her eyes against the darkness, trying to discern if what she'd seen was a trick of light or something more sinister.

The graveyard, once a place of somber reflection, now felt charged with potential danger. Every mausoleum appeared to her as a possible hideout, every statue a silent accomplice to whatever lurked among the graves.

"Come on, Amelia," she muttered under her breath, chiding herself for letting the unease get the better of her. "You've stared down killers without flinching."

But as another flicker of movement disturbed the night, this time closer, she knew that, rational or not, her instincts had been triggered. There was something here with her—a presence that did not belong amidst the solemn rows of the deceased.

And in that moment, Amelia understood that the sign she had asked for was not one of assurance or closure. It was a warning, as tangible as the chill that now crept up her spine.

Amelia's heart raced as the shadows danced with menacing intent, transforming the cemetery into a labyrinth of fear. With each step, the sense of dread coiled tighter around her, like ivy on ancient stone. Grasping for something familiar, something real, she thrust her hand into the pocket of her coat and fumbled for her phone.

"Come on," she whispered to herself, her breath forming clouds in the chilly air. Anxiously, she swiped the screen, searched for Finn's contact, and pressed call. The ringtone, usually a sign of impending support, now seemed absurdly out of place amidst the whispering leaves and watchful angels.

"Pick up, Finn," she murmured, her voice barely above a hush, as if speaking louder would invoke the attention of whatever lurked just beyond sight. Her eyes darted between the headstones, seeking any movement, any hint of what had stirred the stillness of the night.

But the phone call, which should have been her lifeline, was met with silence. A glance at the display confirmed her fears: No Service. The reality of her isolation settled heavily upon her, a cloak woven from threads of vulnerability.

"Damn it." She stuffed the phone back into her coat, her fingers trembling slightly. This wasn't the time to panic; she needed to think like a detective, not a scared civilian. Amelia reminded herself that she'd faced peril before, alongside Finn, their partnership a blend of his methodical approach and her instinct.

In the darkness of the graveyard, though, logic seemed distant, as if muffled by the earth that cradled the silent residents beneath her feet. Here, among the relics of lives long passed, her connection to the world of the living was tenuous—a single thread frayed by the lack of reception.

"Mark, I could use some help right now," she said softly to the headstone, hoping for strength from memories of her lost fiancé. But Mark's silent epitaph offered no comfort, only the stark reminder of mortality etched in stone.

Gathering the remnants of her resolve, Amelia steeled herself against the night's embrace. This was no time for sentiment or fear. She was Inspector Amelia Winters, and she would not be undone by shadows and a signal-less phone.

Amelia's breaths came in shallow gusts, her heart pounding a steady rhythm against her ribs as she navigated the labyrinth of headstones and tombs. She moved with the practiced caution of a detective who had learned to trust her instincts as much as the evidence before her eyes. The moon played peek-a-boo behind scudding clouds, casting a chiaroscuro of light and shadow upon the graves, each one a potential hiding spot for whomever—or whatever—had stirred in the darkness.

She kept her movements measured, her eyes scanning the environment with an intensity borne of years on the force. Each step was deliberate, avoiding the gravel paths that would betray her presence with their telltale crunch underfoot. Instead, she trod upon the grassy spaces between, using the sound of the wind through the trees to cover any inadvertent noise she might make.

A gust sent a shiver down her spine, but Amelia refused to acknowledge it. Fear was a luxury she couldn't afford; fear made you sloppy, and sloppiness got you killed. She thought of Finn, his wry humor a constant through the stormiest cases, how he'd quip about their predicament if he were here now. The thought lent her a modicum of comfort.

Up ahead, the cemetery gates loomed, a silhouette of wrought iron that promised safety and connection to the world beyond this necropolis. Just a few more yards, Amelia told herself, just a few more steps to—

The sudden grip was iron-strong, snatching her from her thoughts and the promise of escape. Before she could react or cry out, she was yanked backward, her feet stumbling over the uneven ground. Panic flared, raw and primal, as she was pulled into the gaping maw of an old tomb, the kind that whispered stories of Victorian mourning and morbid curiosity.

"Let go—" Amelia managed, her voice strangled by the vice-like hold. But her demand was swallowed by the darkness as she was dragged deeper into the crypt, the smell of damp earth and age-old decay filling her lungs. Her training kicked in, and she fought back, twisting in the assailant's grasp, aiming for where she estimated the kidneys would be.

There was no time to think of Mark, of Finn, or of the killer they sought; there was only the here and now, the fight for survival in the clutches of an unknown foe. And as the last sliver of moonlight was blotted out by the closing door of the tomb, Amelia steeled herself for what would come next in the pitch-black embrace of the past.

Amelia's breaths came in short, sharp gasps as she fought against the iron grip of her assailant. She couldn't see his face, but she could feel the malice pouring off him like heat from a fire. The darkness of the tomb closed around her, suffocating and absolute.

"Vilne?" she hissed, trying to make out any feature, any clue that might tell her who had ambushed her in this place of death.

There was no answer, only the sound of her own heart pounding in her ears and the distant hoot of an owl outside. She twisted again, trying to use her elbows, her feet—anything to loosen the vise-like hold. But it was like fighting a shadow, a creature of the night with the strength of the grave itself.

The man pulled and heaved, and Amelia screamed one word as she found herself disappearing into the cold embrace of a tomb.

"Finn!"

CHAPTER TWENTY THREE

The cold, biting air clawed at Finn as he stepped out of the unyielding embrace of his car and into the dark tranquility of Great Amwell. The small village, usually a picture of bucolic charm, now seemed to mock him with its peaceful facade, so starkly opposed to the cacophony of chaos that plagued his mind. His muscles ached from the day's exertions—a relentless pursuit of justice that had culminated in the capture of one suspect only to have another slip through the cracks like water between fingers.

He maneuvered up the cobblestone path leading to his cottage, each step heavy with fatigue. The warmth of the yellow-hued light spilling from his front windows promised solace, but as he fumbled for the keys in his pocket, the optimism was short-lived.

The shrill ring of his mobile phone shattered the night's stillness. Heart leaping to his throat, he fished the device from his coat and squinted against the harsh glow of the screen. Unknown number. With hands that betrayed a tremor, he swiped to answer.

"Detective Finn," came the voice, oily and smooth, a serpent's hiss wrapped in faux cordiality. Max Vilne's tone held an edge of amusement, as if he relished in the disruption of Finn's attempt at respite.

"Vilne," Finn responded, his voice a controlled calm, belying the torrent of dread that surged within. This man, the mastermind behind the chaos that had entangled their lives, was not one to make idle calls.

"Ah, you sound tired, Finn. A long day, I presume?" Vilne's words were a needle, probing for a reaction, seeking to unravel Finn's composure thread by thread.

"Cut to the chase, Vilne," Finn demanded, bracing himself against the frame of his door, the wood's grain pressing into his back. "What do you want?"

"Direct and to the point, I admire that." There was a pause on the line, a momentary silence laden with meaning. "But we'll have plenty of time for pleasantries very soon."

Finn's grip on the phone tightened, knuckles whitening.

The cold night air brushed against Finn's skin as he stepped into his cottage, the unease from the phone call creeping along his spine like tendrils of fog. He had barely made it two steps when Vilne's voice, sardonic and self-assured, slithered through the receiver again.

"Actually, Detective, I'm having a friend over for a late supper," Vilne said, a wolfish grin audible in his tone. "You know how it is, the need for company during these dreary nights."

Finn's jaw clenched, a surge of irritation washing over him. The frivolity with which Vilne treated the situation was infuriating; it was as if they were discussing weather, not lives.

"Who?" Finn demanded, each word clipped like the snap of a whip, though he dreaded the answer.

"Ah, but that would spoil the surprise," Vilne teased, his words laced with malice.

A muffled sound punctured the conversation, a stifled noise that quickly crescendoed into something unmistakable—Amelia's voice, shrill and desperate, pierced the veil of the call. "Finn! Call Rob, get the pol—"

"Amelia!" Finn barked into the phone, his heart hammering against his rib cage, his breath stolen by the raw panic in her voice. He strained to hear more, but there was only the echo of his own shout in the darkness.

"Shh," came Vilne's admonishing whisper, chillingly close to the phone now. "We wouldn't want to make this unpleasant, would we?"

"Vilne, if you hurt her—" Finn began, the threat dying in his throat as the line crackled with the sound of a struggle, Amelia's pleas turning into a cacophony of fear.

"Please, no—Finn, don't give him what he wants!" Her voice broke through once more before being swallowed by a heavy silence.

"Enough games, Vilne," Finn spat, his mind racing, envisioning the layout of the city, every second counting. "What do you want?" His hand tightened on the phone, knuckles going white as he prepared for whatever twisted demand was to come.

"Patience, Detective," Vilne crooned. "All in good time."

Finn's fingers gripped the phone like a lifeline, his other hand flat against the cold kitchen table for balance. The stillness of the cottage amplified the sinister tenor of Vilne's voice as it cut through the silence.

"Let's set one thing straight," Vilne's words slithered from the speaker, "you try to reach out to dear Rob Collins—or any of your police friends—Amelia's last breath will bubble up in dark water."

Finn didn't need to see Vilne's face to know the threat was real; the image of Amelia, thrashing helplessly as dark waters claimed her, flashed cruelly in his mind's eye.

"Listen to me, Vilne," Finn's voice was steel wrapped in velvet, the detective's mind whirring with options, outcomes, angles. "Take me instead. Let Amelia go, and you'll have what you want."

There was a pause on the line, a momentary silence that stretched out like a tightrope. Finn could almost hear the cogs turning in Vilne's twisted mind, calculating, considering. His own heart pounded a frantic rhythm.

"Interesting proposal, Detective," Vilne finally drawled, amusement weaving through his tone. "But do remember, I am not in the habit of negotiating with my... guests."

The raw ache from the blow to Finn's head earlier had settled into a dull throb, a cruel reminder of the day's events and the shadow of Vilne in the crowd. Now, he was being confronted by more than a shadow.

"Come to the Crowmyre factory," Vilne's voice was deceptively calm, an undercurrent of malice bubbling just beneath the surface. "You know the one – ten minutes out from Great Amwell. I thought you should know how close I've been all this time."

The factory, a relic of industrial times now lying dormant, stood like a tombstone for a bygone era. Finn knew it well; a skeletal structure looming against the rural backdrop, its hollowed halls resonating with echoes of its past productivity. It was a fitting stage for a man whose obsession with antiquity bordered on the psychopathic.

"Fine," Finn ground out, his mind racing, every second precious. "But listen here, Vilne. If you so much as—"

"Ah, ah," Vilne interrupted, a smirk audible in his tone. "No conditions, Detective. You're not exactly in a position to negotiate."

Finn's heart was a fist in his chest, pulsing with a cocktail of fury and fear. He pictured Amelia, her determination and unwavering courage in the face of their macabre case. Her life hinged on his next words, his next actions.

"Touch one hair on Amelia's head, and I swear to you," Finn's threat sliced through the line, a razor-sharp promise, "I'll break every bone in your body."

The silence that followed was thick, charged with the weight of his vow. Finn could almost feel Vilne weighing the seriousness of his oath, the potential for retribution.

"Be seeing you, Detective," came the eventual reply, devoid of any warmth.

Finn ended the call, his hands shaking as they clutched at the phone. His pulse hammered in his ears, drowning out the night's gentle whispers. There was no time to waste, no moment to lose.

Finn didn't hesitate. He bolted from the threshold as he rushed toward the kitchen. His mind raced with images of Victorian relics and antique guns, of poisoned darts and the insidious Tempus Machine— but they all paled in comparison to the thought of losing Amelia to a man as ruthless as Max Vilne. How he wished he had his service gun.

In the kitchen, a single bulb cast a stark light over the counter tops Finn's hands moved with purpose, rummaging through drawers with the precision of someone who knew their contents by heart. Cutlery clanked, a discordant melody to his pounding pulse. He needed weapons—crude but effective in close quarters.

His fingers wrapped around the handles of two chef's knives, the blades glinting ominously as he drew them out. They weren't just slabs of metal; to Finn, they were extensions of his will to save Amelia, to end this nightmare that had begun with an ancient computer obsession and led them down London's shadowy paths.

He tested the weight of the knives in his hands, feeling a grim sense of readiness. There would be no fencing with words where he was headed. The Crowmyre factory loomed in his thoughts, a stage set for a final, desperate confrontation.

"Amelia," he whispered, a vow to the darkness. Her name was a talisman against the fear clawing at the edges of his resolve. She'd walked through death's door with him before, had always been the one to keep him grounded in the midst of chaos. He couldn't let her down now.

With the cold steel secured in his grip, Finn turned on his heel, casting one last glance at the quaint cottage that had offered him solace on any other night. But tonight, it was merely a backdrop to the unfolding horror, a brief interlude before the storm.

The knife blades caught the light as he moved, twin promises of protection and vengeance. Finn stepped out of the kitchen, his entire being focused on what lay ahead. Max Vilne and the echoes of his taunting voice awaited him. But in his bones, he he had to fight the weariness. The exhaustion of each injury and wound he had accumulated over the last year in the UK.

Finn's body was a pained coiled spring as he burst through the cottage door, the night air sharp against his flushed skin. The gravel crunched underfoot. His hands were unsteady yet firm as they wrapped around the cold steering wheel of his car. With a swift motion, he ignited the engine, the roar cutting through the quiet countryside like a beacon of his urgency.

CHAPTER TWENTY FOUR

Finn's boots crunched over the detritus that littered the threshold of Crowmyre Factory, an edifice of eroded brick and corroded metal that clawed at the darkening sky like a relic of the industrial age. Its shadowy maw gaped open, the massive doors hanging off rusted hinges, whispering the tales of long-abandoned labor and toil.

Squinting through the dimming light, Finn's instincts prickled as he stepped into the cavernous space, the last rays of sunset filtering through the shattered panes of the high windows. The air was thick with the scent of mold and decay, a testament to centuries of neglect. His breath materialized in cold puffs, the only proof of life in this desolate place.

"FINN!" The shout ricocheted off the crumbling walls, jolting through him with the ferocity of a gunshot. Vilne's voice was unmistakable, a guttural echo that seemed to emerge from every shadow, every hidden corner of the forsaken factory. Finn's hand instinctively went to his belt, feeling for the reassuring weight of the knives he'd secured before leaving his cottage.

"Show yourself, Vilne!" Finn called out, his voice steady despite the pulse hammering in his ears. He advanced cautiously, eyes roving over the darkness that clung to the machinery like cobwebs. Each step took him deeper into the bowels of the building, where history and terror intertwined.

"Come on then, Finn! You're getting colder," taunted Vilne, the twisted amusement evident in his tone. Finn could almost visualize the smirk that would be playing on the man's lips—the same smirk that had haunted him since their last deadly dance in America.

"Let's not play games," Finn retorted, keeping his tone even as he moved toward the source of the sound. The faintest outline of footprints in the dust led him onward, evidence of Vilne's passage. He needed to end this, for Amelia's sake—Inspector Amelia Winters, his partner, whose intellect matched his own and who now faced an unknown fate at the hands of a madman.

"Games?" came Vilne's scoff. "This is no game, detective. This is evolution."

Each word tightened the knot in Finn's chest, knowing that behind Vilne's delusion lay a mind sharp enough to execute whatever twisted plan he had concocted. As he wove between rusting looms and broken conveyor belts, Finn steeled himself for what lay ahead.

"Amelia needs me," he thought, a mantra against the fear that threatened to take hold. She was more than a colleague; she was the one person who understood the demons that drove him, who had seen past the facade of the consultant detective to the man beneath.

"FINN!" Vilne's voice boomed out again, closer now, filled with the dark promise of violence. Finn quickened his pace, his senses on high alert.

"Keep talking," Finn murmured, using the sound of Vilne's voice to guide him through the labyrinth of derelict industry. His fingers curled around the hilt of a knife, ready for the confrontation that was inevitable.

"Always so predictable," Vilne sneered, the words bouncing off the iron and stone.

Finn knew he was right. Vilne always predicted his moves. Finn felt for the three blades wedged down the back of his belt. It was the only protection he had.

The darkness of the Crowmyre Factory seemed to swallow Finn as he moved, a shadow amongst shadows. His breath came in controlled bursts, steeling his nerves against the chill that seeped into his bones. Every echo in the cavernous space was a warning; every drip of water from the decaying rafters was a countdown.

He followed the sound of his name, the syllables stretched and distorted by the ancient brick. The weight of the knives against his thigh was a comfort — a reminder that he was not defenseless against whatever madness awaited him.

"Amelia!" he called out, his voice low, hoping for a response that didn't come.

Then, there she was — Amelia, bound to a chair, her determined eyes meeting his with an unspoken plea. Next to her stood Vilne, a grotesque giant silhouetted against the feeble light, his features twisted into a deranged semblance of joy. Finn's heart clenched at the sight; his partner, his confidant, in the hands of a madman.

"Vilne," Finn spat the name like a curse, feeling the cold air wrap around his tongue.

The large man turned, his smile widening, displaying a row of teeth that gleamed unnaturally in the dimness. "Special Agent," Vilne

140

greeted, a mock formality in his tone. "Or should I say, consulting detective?"

Finn's gaze flickered to the side, noting the soft hum of a generator. It powered a single computer, its screen casting an eerie glow that danced across the walls. The machine looked out of place amidst the decay, a piece of modernity intruding upon the time-ravaged factory.

"Quite the setup you have here," Finn remarked, buying time as his eyes searched for any advantage.

"Efficiency is key," Vilne said, but Finn heard the undercurrent of pride in his voice.

"Let her go, Vilne," Finn demanded, his hand inching toward the hilt of one knife, ready to act on the slightest provocation.

"Ah, but then we'd miss all the fun," Vilne chuckled darkly, his gaze never leaving Finn's.

Finn took a measured step forward, keeping his movements deliberate. "You don't want to do this."

"Contrary to what you might think, detective," Vilne said, stepping closer to the humming computer, "I very much want to do this."

"Your quarrel is with me," Finn countered, locking eyes with Amelia for a brief second, trying to convey a silent message of hope.

"Everything in due time," Vilne replied, his hand hovering over the keyboard. "Every great change begins with a single action."

Finn's mind raced. Whatever plan Vilne had involving that computer, it couldn't be good. He had to find a way to end this before—

"Focus on me, Finn," Vilne commanded, drawing Finn's attention back to him. "Your little sidekick can wait."

"What interest do you have in computer viruses?" Finn asked. "And all of Chronos's Tempus Machine nonsense."

"It's not nonsense," Vilne snapped. "I initially conceived of this as a game to taunt you, but over time I have realized that it can, and should be, much bigger than that."

"Vilne," Finn growled. "What is it that you *really* want?"

With a mad glint in his eye, Vilne pressed the cold steel of a large knife against Amelia's neck. "To make you watch," he hissed.

"Watch what?" Finn demanded, his voice steady despite the panic clawing at his insides.

"Her die," Vilne said simply. "But not before I share my vision."

Finn's gaze snapped to the computer by Vilne's side, the soft blue glow casting sinister shadows across his face. "What madness are you planning?"

"Madness?" Vilne chuckled, a disturbing sound devoid of humor. "No, Detective. It's ambition. A virus, partly my creation, partly Chronos's, partly a few others along the way, ready to send this modern world back to the stone age. Imagine, Finn, all technology rendered useless in an instant."

"You're insane, but you're not that far gone," Finn spat out, barely keeping himself in check. "I don't doubt there is a virus, but what's it really for?

"Insanity is the mother of innovation," Vilne retorted, his eyes alight with fervor. "I will be remembered as the harbinger of a new era. And you, Finn... you'll fail. Not just in saving her," he nodded towards Amelia with a cruel smile, "but in saving your precious modern world, with your influencers and your prisons…"

"I don't believe you... There's more to this..." Finn whispered, every muscle coiled tight, ready to spring.

"Is there?," Vilne said, removing the knife momentarily from Amelia's throat. "Sometimes I think I do things just for the pleasure."

Amelia's eyes remained wide. Finn could see the defiance in them. She wanted Finn to do what he needed to do, regardless of what happened to her. That he knew.

But he couldn't bring himself to see her harmed.

Vilne moved in the darkness like a looming threat, a deranged grin splitting his face as he gestured grandly to the cameras mounted overhead. "Welcome to the show, Detective. The whole world is watching," he proclaimed, his voice tinged with grotesque enthusiasm.

Finn's eyes darted around, taking in the live feed, the cables snaking across the floor to the generator that pulsed with life. "You're streaming this?" he asked, masking his horror with an icy veneer of calm. "Tell me you didn't need help to set up a simple stream? I thought you were a genius. Is that why you were talking with Emily?"

Vilne looked angry for a moment.

"Of course, I didn't need help. I had some correspondence with Henry and Emily, mostly to find whispers of the Tempus Machine so that I could keep Chris Harlow under my thrall. He believed me, the fool."

"You didn't have to kill those people," Finn said.

"You're right. I did it to give you something to do. You should be happy about that. Some of the victims assisted me, not knowing what I was working on. Others were more intimately involved, but it doesn't matter. They were all butchered for *your entertainment*. How love to watch you flounder, Finn! Now... Get this, when *this* stream goes dark, so does the age of technology," Vilne declared triumphantly, his gaze locked onto Finn's with manic intensity. "Oh, I'm sure other computers will be built, perhaps some saved, but not before I've caused utter carnage around the world. Hospital computers, airlines, train terminals, military installations, oh, it's going to be marvelous!"

"I don't buy this," Finn said. "Technology that can delete the internet? Sounds like pie in the sky, but a virus... I believe there is one, but not for the reasons you've said. You lied to Chris Harlow didn't you?"

Vilne looked on, annoyance showing on his face.

"You used him like you used the others," Finn said. "You really are the master manipulator. Even this is a show. If there wasn't a virus, you'd seem inept. You wouldn't have that. Hell, you tracked me down to the UK just to have revenge because I caught you once. No, your pride wouldn't accept the virus being fake, not when you are being watched by God knows how many people."

Vilne smirked to himself.

"So, given what I know about your psychology," Finn continued, "there has to be a virus. But I bet it does something else. What does it do, Max? Tell me, or do you want to win without me ever knowing how clever you've been."

"Well done," Vilne said, calmly. "This virus will infect law enforcement servers across the US. FBI, Homeland, pathetic little Sheriff departments, everything. It will delete every single file, every single record of any crimes and criminals. There will be bedlam, and I will be able to sneak off into the blue. I just wanted to cause a little panic across the way. The entire criminal justice system will collapse with no records of who did what. Mistakes will be expunged, with the added bonus that with no criminal record, I'll be able to use a fake passport and ID to make my way to anywhere in the world I please, and then continue my... Passions..."

Finn laughed. "My God, Vilne. Are you really so pathetic that you need to wipe record of the fact I caught you fair and square."

"There was nothing fair about it!" Vilne readied his hand with the knife. "Now you know the truth. It's been a game, but one where I set the rules. I win. As always. And the world will know it."

"Quite the spectacle you've put together," Finn replied evenly, circling cautiously. He eyed Amelia, bound and resolute despite her predicament, then fixed his stare back on Vilne. "But you see, Vilne, behind all this genius... there's one thing you've overlooked."

"And what would that be?" Vilne sneered, confidence unshaken as he toyed with the knife over Amelia's head.

"Your pride," Finn stated plainly, his voice as sharp as the blades concealed on his person. "It's always been your downfall."

A flicker of irritation crossed Vilne's face before he masked it with a laugh, but Finn saw it—the chink in his armor. With every word, he was gauging, calculating, ready to pounce at the slightest opening. Because this was not just a game of chess; it was a dance with death—and Finn was poised to make his move.

"Ah, but you see, I have no weaknesses, Finn," Vilne snarled, the knife in his hand glinting ominously. "You and your like are too lacking in vision to know this."

"Is that so?" Finn's eyes narrowed. "It was your pride that got you here, wasn't it? Chasing me across the ocean to make a point because I caught you back in the States."

"Respect is what I am due, Finn!" Vilne spat, his eyes wild and fervent. "You were lucky back then. That fire at the hotel—nothing more than a fortunate distraction that let you walk away with Nancy Miller and me, unconscious and in handcuffs."

"Was it luck, or was it your ego overestimating your abilities?" Finn countered with a steady tone, despite the rapid drumming of his pulse. He needed to keep Vilne talking, buy time, look for an opening.

"Luck saved you then," Vilne sneered. "But luck won't save you tonight."

"I suppose I couldn't persuade you to walk away?" Finn's voice reverberated through the empty halls, meeting only shadows.

"You and your jokes," Max said. "I will say, I might miss this back and forth. But all good things must come to an end." He looked at the computer screen. "It's almost uploaded."

"Almost isn't enough," Finn answered.

"You don't even have a gun," Vilne said with venom. "You couldn't best me in a fight a year ago, what makes you think it will be any different tonight?"

"I didn't say it would be different," Finn replied, honing in on his one moment. "But if we're going to dance. I'd rather get to it over all this talking."

"You should be honored to speak with someone with my intellect!" Vilne shouted, raising his hand and knife above Amelia, as if to strike.

"And you should be honored to speak to someone with my aim!"
Finn yelled.

With swift precision, he drew two knives from his belt and flung
them. One spiraled end over end, burying itself deep into Vilne's
shoulder with a sickening thud. Vilne roared, pain and surprise
mingling in his cry, his hulking frame jerking with the impact.

"Amelia!" The name tore from Finn's throat as Vilne, fueled by
fury, brandished his knife at her. Adrenaline surged, narrowing Finn's
world to the blade edging towards Amelia's pale neck.

Time slowed as Finn lunged forward, tackling the looming specter
of death to the side. The knife missed its mark by mere inches, slicing
through the air where Amelia's head had been seconds before. Finn's
hand found the bonds that tethered her to the chair, the ropes biting into
her wrists. With deft movements forged in countless encounters with
death's dance, he sliced through the restraints with his remaining knife,
freeing her.

"Go," he urged, locking eyes with Amelia, her own gaze alight with
a fierce resolve.

"Not without you," she breathed out, steel in her voice matching the
determination in Finn's grip on his remaining knife.

Vilne loomed as large as a stone gargoyle, pulling the knife from
his shoulder. Finn put himself between Vilne and Amelia.

Max Vilne stood, blood oozing from his shoulder, grinning.

"Too late, Finn!" Vilne's voice boomed, reverberating off the
cracked walls. "The virus is already in the system, and you will be the
man who failed *everyone*!"

"Is it?" Finn countered, his tone laced with a dangerous calm as he
glanced at the computer.

The screen was dark, the power light extinguished. A glint of metal
protruded from its side—the second knife embedded deep within its
circuitry. Finn had aimed twice, and hit twice. "You might want to get
someone to look at that, fella. Seems broken to me."

"No!" Vilne shouted.

Amelia stepped beside him, her eyes scanning for any advantage.
"Game over, Vilne."

"The only thing that's over is you!" Vilne's voice crescendoed into a
scream, and he lunged, his large knife cutting through the air with
lethal intent.

Finn reacted instinctively, parrying the blade with his own. Metal clashed against metal, sparks fleeting in the dim light. Amelia moved with precision, aiming to flank their adversary.

Finn gave it his all. He swung, but Vilne dodger, smashing his fist against Finn's side. Finn felt the breath escape from him. Vilne was relentless, catching a punch from Amelia and then slapping her across the face with disdain in his eyes. Vilne surged forward kicking at Finn's knee.

Pain winced up his body. Finn now was no longer on the attack, he had to defend, himself and the woman he loved..

"Upstairs!" Finn shouted to Amelia, nodding toward the dilapidated metal stairs leading to the overhead gangway.

With a mutual understanding born of countless life-or-death moments, they broke away, sprinting up the creaking steps. Finn could feel the rusted metal groan underfoot, threatening to give way at any moment.

Vilne followed, his boots pounding on the stairs like the drumbeat of an ancient war. They reached the gangway, the gridded floor offering a treacherous path as they continued their deadly dance.

"Careful," Finn warned Amelia, his gaze flicking between her and Vilne. "One wrong step..."

"I know," she replied tersely, her focus never wavering from the threat before them.

The gangway swayed slightly, a precarious arena for what could be the final confrontation. Finn could see the crazed determination in Vilne's eyes, the gleam of a man who had nothing left to lose.

"Come on then!" Finn taunted, baiting Vilne, hoping to exploit an opening. "Show us what you've got!"

And with a roar that seemed to shake the very foundations of the Crowmyre Factory, Vilne charged, his knife held high, ready to bring down destruction upon them both.

Finn dodged, and Amelia struck out, but so too did Vilne, kicking her in the side. She fell to the metal railing, slamming against its cold surface, her body careening into a rusted guardrail with a sickening thud. "Amelia!" Finn cried out, but there was no time to aid her.

"Ugh!" she gasped, pain etching her voice, pushing him away with a forceful gesture. Her eyes, usually so full of determination, now flickered with the harsh reality of her injury.

Finn turned back to Vilne. The giant of a man loomed closer, malice seeping from every pore. Finn could feel the years weighing upon him

146

like lead, his senses dulled, his reflexes a fraction too slow. He had relied on wits and old-school cunning in all his cases, but against Vilne's brute strength and unhinged speed, he felt a daunting disadvantage.

"Getting old, Finn?" Vilne mocked, his voice echoing through the abandoned factory. "Can't quite keep up anymore?"

Finn dodged a swipe, the knife's blade glinting perilously close. He parried with one of his own, the familiar grip reassuring against his palm. But Vilne was relentless. Another strike, faster than the last, sent Finn's knife clattering away across the gridded floor.

"Damn it," he muttered under his breath, the cold air filling his lungs as he tried to steady himself.

Vilne lunged again, and this time Finn wasn't quick enough. A heavy blow to his chest sent him sprawling backward, his hands grasping at nothingness as he hit the ground hard. Pain shot through him, his vision blurring at the edges.

"Come on, detective," sneered Vilne, grabbing Finn by the collar and dragging him towards the edge of the gangway. "Let's see the view from up here."

Dangling over open air, Finn's feet kicked futilely, his heart pounding a frantic rhythm. Below, the shadows of ancient machinery loomed, ready to embrace him in their silent graveyard.

"Look at you," Vilne taunted, his breath hot on Finn's face. "No backup. No tricks. Just a washed-up agent playing hero."

"You really are boring," Finn retorted, even as his fingers scrabbled for a hold on the corroded metal.

Vilne's laugh was devoid of humor, a sound that chilled Finn to the core. "Weakness, Finn. It'll be your end. Only now, at the end, do you really how alone you really are. How alone you have *always* been!"

Finn's every breath formed misty clouds in the chill air as his feet dragged against the precarious gangway. Vilne's fingers dug into his collar, the threat of a long fall looming behind him. Yet amid desperation, a defiant spark ignited within.

"Vilne," Finn grated out, "you think you've won because I'm alone. But your real weakness... you'll never understand what it is to have someone watch your back."

At that moment, Amelia emerged like vengeance from the shadows, her presence a sudden burst of hope. With a fierce cry, she delivered a roundhouse kick to Vilne's side. The man stumbled, his grip loosening, giving Finn the chance he needed. He broke free, rolling away to safety.

They stood side by side, facing their foe, who recovered with a snarl. The battle resumed, the clanging of their footsteps echoing through the forsaken factory as they circled Vilne.

The killer swung, and Amelia dodged, grit and determination etched onto her face.

"Enough!" Amelia taunted, catching the man's wrist and twisting it, making Vilne grimace momentarily from the pain, but he then grabbed Amelia viciously by the throat. She gasped for air.

But Amelia's efforts had given Finn enough time to move in.

Summoning strength from deep within, he saw his opening and took it, his fist rocketing upwards in an uppercut that connected with the underside of Vilne's chin. The force of the blow was seismic, freeing Amelia and sending Vilne staggering backward. His foot slipped, his arms windmilling as he tried to catch himself, but there was nothing but air.

With a final look of disbelief etched on his face, Vilne plummeted off the gangway, disappearing into the darkness below with a sound that would haunt the survivors.

"Is it over?" Amelia breathed, leaning heavily against Finn for support.

Finn's breath came in ragged gasps as he slumped against the cold, gritty wall of the Crowmyre Factory. The adrenaline that had fueled his muscles was now a dwindling fire, leaving only ash and exhaustion in its wake. He felt the weight of every bruise and cut, the legacy of the night's grim ballet.

"Easy," Amelia said softly, her presence suddenly beside him. She lowered herself to the ground, her hands gently cradling his head, easing it onto her lap. Her touch was soothing more than she could ever know.

"I guess we've gone global," Finn muttered, his voice betraying the fatigue that threatened to claim him. He pointed up at the cameras Vilne had set up.

"Rest for a moment," she replied, her fingers brushing back a lock of hair matted with sweat from his forehead. "We earned it."

The silence between them was laden with words unsaid, each heartbeat a tick on the metronome of their shared experience. The factory loomed around them, an echo chamber of their confrontation with death, a testament to their victory over darkness.

"Amelia..." Finn began, the urgency in his voice cutting through the quiet.

"I know," she whispered before he could continue. "Me too."

The sirens wailed in the distance, a discordant chorus heralding the approach of law and order, of reality rushing back to fill the void left by chaos. But in that fleeting sanctuary, their world narrowed to the space they occupied, to the truths they had danced around.

"Can we start living now?" Finn said, his eyes searching hers in the dim light, seeking affirmation, seeking solace.

"Try and stop me," Amelia offered, the hint of a smile tugging at the corner of her lips. Her gaze held his, fierce and unwavering.

Outside, the crescendo of sirens grew louder, an insistent reminder of the roles they played, of the duty that awaited them beyond these walls. But within the crumbling confines of the Crowmyre Factory, time seemed to slow, allowing them just a moment longer, a moment where nothing else mattered but the truth laid bare between them.

"Then let's start there," Finn said, finding a strength he didn't know he had left. "I love you, Amelia Winters."

"And I love you, Finn," she replied, her voice steady even as the world outside beckoned them back to reality. "But I am going back to that Pendergast's store to buy all sorts of crazy antiques shenanigans.

Amelia laughed. "As long as it isn't a time machine."

EPILOGUE

The sun was just beginning to crest over the London skyline as Finn Wright and Amelia Winters emerged from the police station, their faces etched with a mixture of exhaustion and relief. The past 24 hours had been a whirlwind of chaos and danger, a desperate race against time to stop a madman and save countless lives. But now, as the city began to stir and the first rays of dawn painted the streets in a soft, golden light, they could finally allow themselves a moment to breathe.

They walked in silence for a while, their footsteps echoing off the cobblestones, each lost in their own thoughts. Finn couldn't quite believe that it was over, that the nightmare that had consumed his every waking moment for the past few weeks had finally come to an end. He felt a strange sense of emptiness as if a part of him had been hollowed out by the experience. But he also felt a newfound sense of purpose, a clarity that had eluded him for so long.

Beside him, Amelia seemed to be grappling with her own emotions. She had been a rock throughout the entire ordeal, a constant source of strength and support, but Finn could see the toll it had taken on her. There were shadows under her eyes and a weariness in her step that hadn't been there before. But there was also a fire in her gaze, a determination that had only grown stronger with each passing day.

As they turned a corner and found themselves in a quiet, secluded square, Finn finally broke the silence.

"I can't believe it's really over," he said softly, his voice barely above a whisper. "I keep expecting to wake up and find out Vilne is still alive."

Amelia let out a small, tired laugh. "I know what you mean," she said, shaking her head. "It doesn't feel real. But we did it, Finn. We stopped him."

Finn nodded, a lump forming in his throat. "We did," he said, his voice rough with emotion. "Usually I'd joke about my handsomeness getting us through it... But I think that only counted for 47% of it."

Amelia's eyes widened, her breath catching in her throat. For a moment, she seemed to struggle for words, her lips moving soundlessly. Then, with a sudden, fierce intensity, she pulled Finn into a searing kiss.

Time seemed to stand still as they lost themselves in each other, the rest of the world falling away until there was nothing but the two of them, the warmth of their bodies pressed together, the pounding of their hearts. When they finally broke apart, breathless and flushed, Finn could see the same love and desire mirrored in Amelia's eyes that he felt in his own heart.

"I love you, Finn Wright," Amelia said, her voice trembling with emotion. "I think I've loved you from the moment we first met. I was just too stubborn to admit it."

Finn felt a wave of joy and relief wash over him, a sense of rightness that he had never experienced before. "I love you too, Amelia Winters," he said, his voice cracking with the weight of his feelings. "And I promise, from this moment on, I will never let you go."

"No jokes this time?" Amelia smiled.

"I *can* be serious, you know."

They stood there for a long time, wrapped in each other's arms, savoring the moment of peace and connection. But eventually, the outside world began to intrude once more, the sounds of the city growing louder as the morning rush began.

Just as they were about to head back to the station, Finn's phone buzzed in his pocket. He pulled it out, surprised to see the name of his old FBI boss, Director Seward, flashing on the screen.

With a puzzled frown, he answered the call. "Director Seward," he said, his voice cautious. "What can I do for you?"

There was a moment of silence on the other end of the line, then a gruff, familiar voice spoke. "Finn," Seward said, his tone uncharacteristically gentle. "That live stream went viral. I just got a full report about what happened in London. About Vilne, and the case you've been working on. It's all over the press in the US."

Finn felt a flicker of apprehension, wondering if this was the moment when his past would finally catch up with him. But Seward's next words put those fears to rest.

"I wanted to let you know that the Bureau is dropping the investigation into your actions," Seward said, his voice firm and decisive. "And... An independent insurance investigation has found that the hotel was a fire trap, so the damage wasn't all your fault during the the hostage situation a year ago.

"In light of Vilne's escape from US custody and the role you played in bringing him to justice in the UK, and from stopping that virus from… Well, it doesn't bear thinking. It's clear that you acted in the best interests of the public and the Bureau. You're a damn fine agent, Finn, and we're lucky to have you. I'm just sorry it took all of this to make that clear, those fools above me."

Finn felt a rush of emotions - relief, gratitude, and a strange sense of closure. He had spent so long running from his past, from the mistakes he had made and the bridges he had burned. But now, it seemed, he could finally put those ghosts to rest.

"Thank you, sir," he said, his voice thick with emotion. "That means a lot, coming from you."

Seward cleared his throat, a hint of awkwardness creeping into his voice. "Yes, well," he said gruffly. "I know things haven't always been easy between us, Finn. But I want you to know that I've always respected your talent and your dedication. Your job is safe here at the Bureau."

Finn felt a smile tugging at his lips, a sense of warmth and appreciation flooding through him. But even as he savored the moment, he knew in his heart that his path lay elsewhere.

"I appreciate that, sir," he said, his voice steady and sure. "But I'm afraid I won't be coming back to the Bureau. I've found a new home here in London, a new purpose. And I have people here who need me, who I can't leave behind."

He glanced over at Amelia, who was watching him with a curious, expectant expression. "I have a partner here who means the world to me," he said softly, his eyes never leaving hers. "And I have friends who have become like family. I can't imagine leaving them now, not after everything we've been through together."

There was a long, thoughtful pause on the other end of the line. Then, to Finn's surprise, Seward let out a low, rumbling chuckle.

"I had a feeling you might say that," he said, a note of amusement in his voice. "And I can't say I blame you. From what I've heard, you've built quite a life for yourself over there. And if there's one thing I've learned in this job, it's that family is the most important thing there is."

Finn felt a rush of gratitude and affection for his old boss, a man who had been a mentor and a friend, even when their relationship had been strained. "Thank you, sir," he said, his voice thick with emotion. "For everything."

"Take care of yourself, Finn," Seward said, his voice gruff but sincere. "And know that you'll always have a friend at the Bureau, no matter where you are. If you're ever back in the States, let's go fishing like we used to."

With that, the call ended, leaving Finn feeling strangely lighter, as if a weight had been lifted from his shoulders. He turned to Amelia, a broad smile spreading across his face.

"That was my old boss at the FBI," he said, tucking his phone back into his pocket. "They're dropping the investigation into my actions. And he offered me my old job back."

Amelia's eyes widened, a flicker of fear and uncertainty crossing her face. "What did you tell him?" she asked, her voice barely above a whisper.

Finn reached out and took her hand, his fingers intertwining with hers. "I told him no," he said softly, his eyes shining with love and conviction. "I told him that my home is here now, with you and Rob and the rest of the team. And that there's nowhere else I'd rather be."

Amelia's face broke into a radiant smile, her eyes brimming with tears of joy and relief. She threw her arms around Finn, holding him close as if she never wanted to let go.

"I won't tell you I love you again," she whispered, her voice muffled against his chest. "I don't want you to grow tired of it."

Finn held her tight, his heart swelling with a love and happiness he had never known before. "I'm free now," he murmured, pressing a kiss to the top of her head. "Free of all the weight of that damned case. Free to do what *we* want to do."

They stayed like that for a long moment, wrapped in each other's arms, savoring the warmth and comfort of their embrace. But eventually, they knew they had to face the world once more.

Hand in hand, they made their way back to the station, ready to face whatever challenges lay ahead. They knew that there would be new cases to solve, new mysteries to unravel, and new dangers to confront. But they also knew that they had each other, and that was enough.

As they walked through the doors of the station, they were greeted by a sea of familiar faces - Rob, grinning from ear to ear; the rest of the team, applauding and cheering their success; and even a few of the journalists who had been covering the case, eager for a final word from the heroes of the hour.

"I know you don't want to hear this," Rob said. "But the Home office wants to start a new division with the three of us. It could be quite the adventure?"

"I'm in," Finn said.

"So am I," agreed Amelia.

"But first," Rob said. "Why don't you both take a month off and... Erm... Get to know each other a bit more."

"Thanks, Rob," Finn said. Rob patted him on the arm and walked away, back to the crowd of people gathering.

Finn and Amelia smiled and waved, basking in the warm glow of their victory. But even as they savored the moment, they knew that their work was far from over.

There would always be darkness in the world, always be those who sought to harm and destroy. But as long as there were people like Finn, Amelia, and Rob, people who were willing to stand up and fight for what was right, there would also be hope.

NOW AVAILABLE!

NOT THIS WAY
(A Rachel Blackwood Suspense Thriller—Book One)

Texas Ranger (and part Native American) Rachel Blackwood, fierce and resilient, must cross the harsh Texas landscape, tracking the most notorious serial killers. But when a killer surfaces deep in oil country, Rachel realizes she is up against she has never seen before…

"A masterpiece of thriller and mystery."
—Books and Movie Reviews, Roberto Mattos (re Once Gone)

NOT THIS WAY (A Rachel Blackwood Suspense Thriller—Book 1) is Book #1 in a long-anticipated new series by #1 bestseller and USA Today bestselling author Blake Pierce, whose bestseller *The Perfect Wife* (a free download) has received over 20,000 five star reviews.

As a child, Rachel felt a connection to her Native American heritage, learning traditional customs and survival skills from the aunt who raised her. Haunted for years by her parents' mysterious and unsolved deaths, Rachel vowed to find their killer—and protect all other innocent lives from the same fate.
Can Rachel find the killer in time before he strikes again?

A page-turning and harrowing suspense thriller featuring a brilliant and tortured protagonist, the RACHEL BLACKWOOD series is a riveting mystery, packed with suspense, twists and turns, revelations, and driven by a breakneck pace that will keep you flipping pages late into the night.

Future books in the series are also available.

"An edge of your seat thriller in a new series that keeps you turning pages! ...So many twists, turns and red herrings... I can't wait to see what happens next."
—Reader review (Her Last Wish)

"A strong, complex story about two FBI agents trying to stop a serial killer. If you want an author to capture your attention and have you guessing, yet trying to put the pieces together, Pierce is your author!"
—Reader review (Her Last Wish)

"A typical Blake Pierce twisting, turning, roller coaster ride suspense thriller. Will have you turning the pages to the last sentence of the last chapter!!!"
—Reader review (City of Prey)

"Right from the start we have an unusual protagonist that I haven't seen done in this genre before. The action is nonstop… A very atmospheric novel that will keep you turning pages well into the wee hours."
—Reader review (City of Prey)

"Everything that I look for in a book… a great plot, interesting characters, and grabs your interest right away. The book moves along at a breakneck pace and stays that way until the end. Now on go I to book two!"
—Reader review (Girl, Alone)

"Exciting, heart pounding, edge of your seat book… a must read for mystery and suspense readers!"
—Reader review (Girl, Alone)

Blake Pierce

Blake Pierce is the USA Today bestselling author of the RILEY PAGE mystery series, which includes seventeen books. Blake Pierce is also the author of the MACKENZIE WHITE mystery series, comprising fourteen books; of the AVERY BLACK mystery series, comprising six books; of the KERI LOCKE mystery series, comprising five books; of the MAKING OF RILEY PAIGE mystery series, comprising six books; of the KATE WISE mystery series, comprising seven books; of the CHLOE FINE psychological suspense mystery, comprising six books; of the JESSIE HUNT psychological suspense thriller series, comprising thirty-eight books (and counting); of the AU PAIR psychological suspense thriller series, comprising three books; of the ZOE PRIME mystery series, comprising six books; of the ADELE SHARP mystery series, comprising sixteen books, of the EUROPEAN VOYAGE cozy mystery series, comprising six books; of the LAURA FROST FBI suspense thriller, comprising eleven books; of the ELLA DARK FBI suspense thriller, comprising twenty-one books (and counting); of the A YEAR IN EUROPE cozy mystery series, comprising nine books, of the AVA GOLD mystery series, comprising six books; of the RACHEL GIFT mystery series, comprising fifteen books (and counting); of the VALERIE LAW mystery series, comprising nine books; of the PAIGE KING mystery series, comprising eight books; of the MAY MOORE mystery series, comprising eleven books; of the CORA SHIELDS mystery series, comprising eight books; of the NICKY LYONS mystery series, comprising eight books, of the CAMI LARK mystery series, comprising ten books; of the AMBER YOUNG mystery series, comprising eight books; of the DAISY FORTUNE mystery series, comprising five books; of the FIONA RED mystery series, comprising thirteen books (and counting); of the FAITH BOLD mystery series, comprising seventeen books (and counting); of the JULIETTE HART mystery series, comprising five books; of the MORGAN CROSS mystery series, comprising thirteen books (and counting); of the FINN WRIGHT mystery series, comprising seven books (and counting); of the SHEILA STONE suspense thriller series, comprising eight books (and counting); of the RACHEL BLACKWOOD suspense thriller series, comprising eight books (and counting); and of the new THE

GOVERNESS psychological suspense thriller series, comprising five books (and counting).

An avid reader and lifelong fan of the mystery and thriller genres, Blake loves to hear from you, so please feel free to visit www.blakepierceauthor.com to learn more and stay in touch.

BOOKS BY BLAKE PIERCE

THE GOVERNESS PSYCHOLOGICAL SUSPENSE
ONE LAST LIE (Book #1)
ONE LAST SMILE (Book #2)
ONE LAST BREATH (Book #3)
ONE LAST GOODBYE (Book #4)
ONE LAST SECRET (Book #5)

RACHEL BLACKWOOD SUSPENSE THRILLER
NOT THIS WAY (Book #1)
NOT THIS TIME (Book #2)
NOT THIS CLOSE (Book #3)
NOT THIS ROAD (Book #4)
NOT THIS LATE (Book #5)
NOT THIS NIGHT (Book #6)
NOT THIS PLACE (Book #7)
NOT THIS SOON (Book #8)

SHEILA STONE SUSPENSE THRILLER
SILENT GIRL (Book #1)
SILENT TRAIL (Book #2)
SILENT NIGHT (Book #3)
SILENT HOUSE (Book #4)
SILENT SCREAM (Book #5)
SILENT PREY (Book #6)
SILENT RITUAL (Book #7)
SILENT PRAYER (Book #8)

FINN WRIGHT MYSTERY SERIES
WHEN YOU'RE MINE (Book #1)
WHEN YOU'RE SAFE (Book #2)
WHEN YOU'RE CLOSE (Book #3)
WHEN YOU'RE SLEEPING (Book #4)
WHEN YOU'RE SANE (Book #5)
WHEN YOU'RE SILENT (Book #6)
WHEN YOU'RE GONE (Book #7)

MORGAN CROSS MYSTERY SERIES
FOR YOU (Book #1)
FOR RAGE (Book #2)
FOR LUST (Book #3)
FOR WRATH (Book #4)
FOREVER (Book #5)
FOR US (Book #6)
FOR NOW (Book #7)
FOR ONCE (Book #8)
FOR ETERNITY (Book #9)
FORLORN (Book #10)
FOR SILENCE (Book #11)
FORBIDDEN (Book #12)
FOR FEAR (Book #13)
FORSAKEN (Book #14)

JULIETTE HART MYSTERY SERIES
NOTHING TO FEAR (Book #1)
NOTHING THERE (Book #2)
NOTHING WATCHING (Book #3)
NOTHING HIDING (Book #4)
NOTHING LEFT (Book #5)

FAITH BOLD MYSTERY SERIES
SO LONG (Book #1)
SO COLD (Book #2)
SO SCARED (Book #3)
SO NORMAL (Book #4)
SO FAR GONE (Book #5)
SO LOST (Book #6)
SO ALONE (Book #7)
SO FORGOTTEN (Book #8)
SO INSANE (Book #9)
SO SMITTEN (Book #10)
SO SIMPLE (Book #11)
SO BROKEN (Book #12)
SO CRUEL (Book #13)
SO HAUNTED (Book #14)
SO SILENT (Book #15)

SO BLEAK (Book #16)
SO HOLLOW (Book #17)

FIONA RED MYSTERY SERIES
LET HER GO (Book #1)
LET HER BE (Book #2)
LET HER HOPE (Book #3)
LET HER WISH (Book #4)
LET HER LIVE (Book #5)
LET HER RUN (Book #6)
LET HER HIDE (Book #7)
LET HER BELIEVE (Book #8)
LET HER FORGET (Book #9)
LET HER TRY (Book #10)
LET HER PLAY (Book #11)
LET HER VANISH (Book #12)
LET HER FADE (Book #13)

DAISY FORTUNE MYSTERY SERIES
NEED YOU (Book #1)
CLAIM YOU (Book #2)
CRAVE YOU (Book #3)
CHOOSE YOU (Book #4)
CHASE YOU (Book #5)

AMBER YOUNG MYSTERY SERIES
ABSENT PITY (Book #1)
ABSENT REMORSE (Book #2)
ABSENT FEELING (Book #3)
ABSENT MERCY (Book #4)
ABSENT REASON (Book #5)
ABSENT SANITY (Book #6)
ABSENT LIFE (Book #7)
ABSENT HUMANITY (Book #8)

CAMI LARK MYSTERY SERIES
JUST ME (Book #1)
JUST OUTSIDE (Book #2)
JUST RIGHT (Book #3)
JUST FORGET (Book #4)

JUST ONCE (Book #5)
JUST HIDE (Book #6)
JUST NOW (Book #7)
JUST HOPE (Book #8)
JUST LEAVE (Book #9)
JUST TONIGHT (Book #10)

NICKY LYONS MYSTERY SERIES
ALL MINE (Book #1)
ALL HIS (Book #2)
ALL HE SEES (Book #3)
ALL ALONE (Book #4)
ALL FOR ONE (Book #5)
ALL HE TAKES (Book #6)
ALL FOR ME (Book #7)
ALL IN (Book #8)

CORA SHIELDS MYSTERY SERIES
UNDONE (Book #1)
UNWANTED (Book #2)
UNHINGED (Book #3)
UNSAID (Book #4)
UNGLUED (Book #5)
UNSTABLE (Book #6)
UNKNOWN (Book #7)
UNAWARE (Book #8)

MAY MOORE SUSPENSE THRILLER
NEVER RUN (Book #1)
NEVER TELL (Book #2)
NEVER LIVE (Book #3)
NEVER HIDE (Book #4)
NEVER FORGIVE (Book #5)
NEVER AGAIN (Book #6)
NEVER LOOK BACK (Book #7)
NEVER FORGET (Book #8)
NEVER LET GO (Book #9)
NEVER PRETEND (Book #10)
NEVER HESITATE (Book #11)

PAIGE KING MYSTERY SERIES
THE GIRL HE PINED (Book #1)
THE GIRL HE CHOSE (Book #2)
THE GIRL HE TOOK (Book #3)
THE GIRL HE WISHED (Book #4)
THE GIRL HE CROWNED (Book #5)
THE GIRL HE WATCHED (Book #6)
THE GIRL HE WANTED (Book #7)
THE GIRL HE CLAIMED (Book #8)

VALERIE LAW MYSTERY SERIES
NO MERCY (Book #1)
NO PITY (Book #2)
NO FEAR (Book #3)
NO SLEEP (Book #4)
NO QUARTER (Book #5)
NO CHANCE (Book #6)
NO REFUGE (Book #7)
NO GRACE (Book #8)
NO ESCAPE (Book #9)

RACHEL GIFT MYSTERY SERIES
HER LAST WISH (Book #1)
HER LAST CHANCE (Book #2)
HER LAST HOPE (Book #3)
HER LAST FEAR (Book #4)
HER LAST CHOICE (Book #5)
HER LAST BREATH (Book #6)
HER LAST MISTAKE (Book #7)
HER LAST DESIRE (Book #8)
HER LAST REGRET (Book #9)
HER LAST HOUR (Book #10)
HER LAST SHOT (Book #11)
HER LAST PRAYER (Book #12)
HER LAST LIE (Book #13)
HER LAST WHISPER (Book #14)
HER LAST SECRET (Book #15)

AVA GOLD MYSTERY SERIES
CITY OF PREY (Book #1)

CITY OF FEAR (Book #2)
CITY OF BONES (Book #3)
CITY OF GHOSTS (Book #4)
CITY OF DEATH (Book #5)
CITY OF VICE (Book #6)

A YEAR IN EUROPE
A MURDER IN PARIS (Book #1)
DEATH IN FLORENCE (Book #2)
VENGEANCE IN VIENNA (Book #3)
A FATALITY IN SPAIN (Book #4)

ELLA DARK FBI SUSPENSE THRILLER
GIRL, ALONE (Book #1)
GIRL, TAKEN (Book #2)
GIRL, HUNTED (Book #3)
GIRL, SILENCED (Book #4)
GIRL, VANISHED (Book 5)
GIRL ERASED (Book #6)
GIRL, FORSAKEN (Book #7)
GIRL, TRAPPED (Book #8)
GIRL, EXPENDABLE (Book #9)
GIRL, ESCAPED (Book #10)
GIRL, HIS (Book #11)
GIRL, LURED (Book #12)
GIRL, MISSING (Book #13)
GIRL, UNKNOWN (Book #14)
GIRL, DECEIVED (Book #15)
GIRL, FORLORN (Book #16)
GIRL, REMADE (Book #17)
GIRL, BETRAYED (Book #18)
GIRL, BOUND (Book #19)
GIRL, REFORMED (Book #20)
GIRL, REBORN (Book #21)

LAURA FROST FBI SUSPENSE THRILLER
ALREADY GONE (Book #1)
ALREADY SEEN (Book #2)
ALREADY TRAPPED (Book #3)
ALREADY MISSING (Book #4)

ALREADY DEAD (Book #5)
ALREADY TAKEN (Book #6)
ALREADY CHOSEN (Book #7)
ALREADY LOST (Book #8)
ALREADY HIS (Book #9)
ALREADY LURED (Book #10)
ALREADY COLD (Book #11)

EUROPEAN VOYAGE COZY MYSTERY SERIES
MURDER (AND BAKLAVA) (Book #1)
DEATH (AND APPLE STRUDEL) (Book #2)
CRIME (AND LAGER) (Book #3)
MISFORTUNE (AND GOUDA) (Book #4)
CALAMITY (AND A DANISH) (Book #5)
MAYHEM (AND HERRING) (Book #6)

ADELE SHARP MYSTERY SERIES
LEFT TO DIE (Book #1)
LEFT TO RUN (Book #2)
LEFT TO HIDE (Book #3)
LEFT TO KILL (Book #4)
LEFT TO MURDER (Book #5)
LEFT TO ENVY (Book #6)
LEFT TO LAPSE (Book #7)
LEFT TO VANISH (Book #8)
LEFT TO HUNT (Book #9)
LEFT TO FEAR (Book #10)
LEFT TO PREY (Book #11)
LEFT TO LURE (Book #12)
LEFT TO CRAVE (Book #13)
LEFT TO LOATHE (Book #14)
LEFT TO HARM (Book #15)
LEFT TO RUIN (Book #16)

THE AU PAIR SERIES
ALMOST GONE (Book#1)
ALMOST LOST (Book #2)
ALMOST DEAD (Book #3)

ZOE PRIME MYSTERY SERIES

FACE OF DEATH (Book#1)
FACE OF MURDER (Book #2)
FACE OF FEAR (Book #3)
FACE OF MADNESS (Book #4)
FACE OF FURY (Book #5)
FACE OF DARKNESS (Book #6)

A JESSIE HUNT PSYCHOLOGICAL SUSPENSE SERIES
THE PERFECT WIFE (Book #1)
THE PERFECT BLOCK (Book #2)
THE PERFECT HOUSE (Book #3)
THE PERFECT SMILE (Book #4)
THE PERFECT LIE (Book #5)
THE PERFECT LOOK (Book #6)
THE PERFECT AFFAIR (Book #7)
THE PERFECT ALIBI (Book #8)
THE PERFECT NEIGHBOR (Book #9)
THE PERFECT DISGUISE (Book #10)
THE PERFECT SECRET (Book #11)
THE PERFECT FAÇADE (Book #12)
THE PERFECT IMPRESSION (Book #13)
THE PERFECT DECEIT (Book #14)
THE PERFECT MISTRESS (Book #15)
THE PERFECT IMAGE (Book #16)
THE PERFECT VEIL (Book #17)
THE PERFECT INDISCRETION (Book #18)
THE PERFECT RUMOR (Book #19)
THE PERFECT COUPLE (Book #20)
THE PERFECT MURDER (Book #21)
THE PERFECT HUSBAND (Book #22)
THE PERFECT SCANDAL (Book #23)
THE PERFECT MASK (Book #24)
THE PERFECT RUSE (Book #25)
THE PERFECT VENEER (Book #26)
THE PERFECT PEOPLE (Book #27)
THE PERFECT WITNESS (Book #28)
THE PERFECT APPEARANCE (Book #29)
THE PERFECT TRAP (Book #30)
THE PERFECT EXPRESSION (Book #31)
THE PERFECT ACCOMPLICE (Book #32)

THE PERFECT SHOW (Book #33)
THE PERFECT POISE (Book #34)
THE PERFECT CROWD (Book #35)
THE PERFECT CRIME (Book #36)
THE PERFECT PREY (Book #37)
THE PERFECT BETRAYAL (Book #38)

CHLOE FINE PSYCHOLOGICAL SUSPENSE SERIES
NEXT DOOR (Book #1)
A NEIGHBOR'S LIE (Book #2)
CUL DE SAC (Book #3)
SILENT NEIGHBOR (Book #4)
HOMECOMING (Book #5)
TINTED WINDOWS (Book #6)

KATE WISE MYSTERY SERIES
IF SHE KNEW (Book #1)
IF SHE SAW (Book #2)
IF SHE RAN (Book #3)
IF SHE HID (Book #4)
IF SHE FLED (Book #5)
IF SHE FEARED (Book #6)
IF SHE HEARD (Book #7)

THE MAKING OF RILEY PAIGE SERIES
WATCHING (Book #1)
WAITING (Book #2)
LURING (Book #3)
TAKING (Book #4)
STALKING (Book #5)
KILLING (Book #6)

RILEY PAIGE MYSTERY SERIES
ONCE GONE (Book #1)
ONCE TAKEN (Book #2)
ONCE CRAVED (Book #3)
ONCE LURED (Book #4)
ONCE HUNTED (Book #5)
ONCE PINED (Book #6)
ONCE FORSAKEN (Book #7)

ONCE COLD (Book #8)
ONCE STALKED (Book #9)
ONCE LOST (Book #10)
ONCE BURIED (Book #11)
ONCE BOUND (Book #12)
ONCE TRAPPED (Book #13)
ONCE DORMANT (Book #14)
ONCE SHUNNED (Book #15)
ONCE MISSED (Book #16)
ONCE CHOSEN (Book #17)

MACKENZIE WHITE MYSTERY SERIES
BEFORE HE KILLS (Book #1)
BEFORE HE SEES (Book #2)
BEFORE HE COVETS (Book #3)
BEFORE HE TAKES (Book #4)
BEFORE HE NEEDS (Book #5)
BEFORE HE FEELS (Book #6)
BEFORE HE SINS (Book #7)
BEFORE HE HUNTS (Book #8)
BEFORE HE PREYS (Book #9)
BEFORE HE LONGS (Book #10)
BEFORE HE LAPSES (Book #11)
BEFORE HE ENVIES (Book #12)
BEFORE HE STALKS (Book #13)
BEFORE HE HARMS (Book #14)

AVERY BLACK MYSTERY SERIES
CAUSE TO KILL (Book #1)
CAUSE TO RUN (Book #2)
CAUSE TO HIDE (Book #3)
CAUSE TO FEAR (Book #4)
CAUSE TO SAVE (Book #5)
CAUSE TO DREAD (Book #6)

KERI LOCKE MYSTERY SERIES
A TRACE OF DEATH (Book #1)
A TRACE OF MURDER (Book #2)
A TRACE OF VICE (Book #3)
A TRACE OF CRIME (Book #4)

A TRACE OF HOPE (Book #5)

Made in the USA
Las Vegas, NV
19 December 2024